A
Reason
to Be Here

A
Reason
to Be Here

Tales from the Writers Convention

A collaborative novel by authors from the
Off Campus Writers Workshop

Conceived and Edited by Jay Rehak

WINDY CITY
PUBLISHERS

A Reason to Be Here

Tales from the Writers Convention

Windy City Publishers
2118 Plum Grove Road, #349
Rolling Meadows, IL 60008
www.windycitypublishers.com

Published in the United States of America

ISBN:
978-1-941478-78-3

Library of Congress Control Number:
2019937919

Cover Image:
Claudio Ventrella © 123RF.com

WINDY CITY PUBLISHERS
CHICAGO

We dedicate this novel to the pioneering women
who created Off Campus Writers Workshop in 1946.
In so doing, they made possible a great many books, poems,
memoirs, and short stories that have been authored by people like us,
who found in OCWW a vehicle to pursue their writing dreams.

Here are the founding members we have been able to identify so far.

Louise Christopher (Chairman)

Rita Turow

Laura Nance

Alice Strauss

Carol Spelius

Fern Brown

Virginia Wilcox

Mary Farnum

Prentiss McKenzie

Mildred Main

Louise B. Buck

Gail B. Burket

Priscilla Chapin

About Off Campus Writers Workshop

Off Campus Writers Workshop is Metro Chicago's Premier Writing Group and the longest continuously running program of its type in the United States.

It was founded in 1946 by a dozen wives of Northwestern professors who sought to establish a haven for themselves to enjoy communal writing and socialization separate from their husbands' work interests.

Many of the founding members were accomplished journalists, short story writers, memoirists, and essayists, while others wrote purely for personal pleasure. Each desired to build upon and improve their craft. Rita Turow, an accomplished writer in her own right, and mother of Scott Turow, the *New York Times* best-selling mystery author, was one of OCWW's founding members.

OCWW offers author/teacher-led instructional writing workshops on Thursdays from September through May. Most sessions are held in the morning at the Winnetka Community House, 620 Lincoln Avenue, Winnetka, Illinois, from 9:30 am to noon. OCWW also conducts some evening sessions at alternate locations.

Summer programming is limited to members only and consists of informal "prompt" and "critique" sessions.

OCWW speakers address writers on topics ranging from craft, to publishing options, to the business of writing. Many of our speakers offer professional manuscript critiques for a nominal fee. Members and guests can achieve their individual writing goals while enjoying the camaraderie and support of fellow writers. The organization's writing programs serve writers of all genres and all levels of accomplishment, from those just learning the craft to published authors of many books.

Learn more about OCWW at our web site, https://ocww.info/.

Contents

xiii   Foreword

xv   Acknowledgments

chapter 1

1   The Decision to Attend by Jay Rehak
What matters when adulation becomes passé?

chapter 2

7   The Haircut by Elizabeth DeSchryver
A girl's rebellion triggers revelations from her
stern grandmother.

chapter 3

15   I've Got Your Number by Adrianne Hayward
Nore faces hard choices after falling in love with a
married man.

chapter 4

21   The Last Word by Hollie Smurthwaite
Lania struggles to accept her past.

chapter 5

27   Killing Teddy by Renee James
A transgender child goes swimming with a bully.

chapter 6

35 **The Healer** by Tonya Coats
Racial put-downs help an African-American woman
accept her destiny.

chapter 7

41 **Between the Lines** by Lyssa Menard
Erin's precocious publishing success masks the
meaning of her words.

chapter 8

49 **The Play** by Melissa Ann Weidner
A young addict sees her life in a stage play.

chapter 9

55 **Hal's Story** by Thomas Sundell
Young Hal's father walks out on the family.

chapter 10

61 **The Pacifist** by Susan Levi
A young girl's self-concept is challenged by a fight
with her best friend.

chapter 11

67 **Gabriel Bryant Bruce** by Michael Farley
A litter of words left behind.

chapter 12

75 **Alpha Dog** by Teri Lavelle
A rambunctious dog humiliates thirteen-year-old Megan.

chapter 13

81 **Wishing Well** by Paco Aramburu
A man's destiny is changed by an odd passenger.

chapter 14

89 Millie by Fred Fitzsimmons
A great short story writer's dying wish.

chapter 15

95 Memories Awakened by Cathy Chester
A homeless woman cuts to the truth in Cindi's life.

chapter 16

101 The Week That Was by Della Leavitt
A teen-ager's first trip to New York during a world-changing week.

chapter 17

107 Welcome Home by Lisa Sukenic
Dora's life begins with an escape from Nazi Europe.

chapter 18

113 Sylvie Green by Deborah Kahn
Sylvie deals with self-esteem issues.

chapter 19

121 The Yearbook by Susan Winstead
Saving the high school yearbook was just the start.

chapter 20

127 The Break-In by Dorothy de Souza Guedes
Lydia's life changes after a cabin break-in.

chapter 21

137 The Oklahoman by Jason Lavicky
William Cordial tries to fit into a new culture.

chapter 22

143 The Big Lie by Patricia Skalka
A childhood lie informs a writer's life.

chapter 23

151

Dr. Edgar Hochstein by Emmet Hirsch
The brilliant and arrogant Hochstein isn't all he appears to be.

chapter 24

157

Persistence of Memory by Joan Naper
Kathy's childhood friendships come alive in her stories.

chapter 25

163

Beyond Death by Susan Van Dusen
A woman in black tells Alice a story.

chapter 26

169

Tango by Judy Panko Reis
An unreliable friend needs one last favor.

chapter 27

175

Getting What She Wanted by Jay Rehak
Alice reflects on all she has learned at the conference.

183   About Jay Rehak

Foreword

In the early days of 2013, the Chicago Writers Association recognized a collaborative novel written by a class of high school seniors as its book of the year in the Indie fiction category.

Thirty Days to Empathy is believed to have been the first-ever collaborative novel written by high schoolers, and it was the first such book to be honored by CWA. It tells the story of a brilliant and arrogant high school senior who is challenged by the only teacher he respects to develop a little empathy for his classmates, some of whom must overcome severe challenges just to get to school each day. Through a bit of magical realism, the student subsequently awakens each day thereafter in the body of a different classmate and spends a day living that classmate's life.

One of the judges who read *Thirty Days to Empathy* was Renee James, a member of the Off Campus Writers Workshop. James found the novel powerfully moving and has recommended it to many friends and colleagues in the years since. James works with OCWW's Susan Levi to recruit and schedule the group's weekly lectures on creative writing, and they discussed approaching Jay Rehak, the Chicago public school teacher who spearheaded the *Empathy* project, to lead an OCWW team in a collaborative novel venture. They brought the idea to the OCWW board, which approved it, and here we are.

Jay Rehak's impressive biography appears elsewhere in this volume, but suffice it to say, he has literally written the book on collaborative novel writing: *How to Write a Class-Sourced Novel* by Jay Rehak is available on Amazon.

While Jay's inspiration originally focused on high school students, the concept proved popular and fulfilling for the adult writers who populate the Off Campus Writers Workshop. In this, our first such project, twenty-five members stepped forward to make the commitment to this project. Not a single one dropped out. No one missed a deadline. The enthusiasm for the project has been high from the start.

Our twenty-five authors comprise a full range of fiction-writing experience. Our numbers include everything from award-winning authors with many publishing credits to those who have finally found moments in their demanding lives to begin learning the arts of story-telling and creative writing. Our stories deal with the kind of conflicts that help to shape a life. Some are dark, some triumphant, but they are as varied as the authors themselves.

Along with our mentor, editor, and leader, Jay Rehak, all twenty-five of us invite you into the pages of *A Reason to Be Here*. We hope you enjoy our stories.

Acknowledgments

Books like this aren't possible without help from many volunteers. In addition to the people who authored pieces for *A Reason to Be Here*, we thank those who stepped forward to do the grunt work involved in publication: Jay Rehak, for his brilliant editing of every story; Renee James, for her initial edits on every story; Fred Fitzsimmons, for his research of OCWW's founders and book launch planning; Lise Marinelli and Dawn McGarrahan Wiebe of Windy City Publishers, for producing this book; Della Leavitt, Thomas Sundell, Emmet Hirsch, Melissa Weidner, and Tonya Coats, for proofreading our breathless prose; Jason Lavicky, for his help with production oversight; Hollie Smurthwaite, for her research on titles and cover images for the book; and Paco Aramburu, for his cover ideas and book launch planning.

The authors of Off Campus Writers Workshop would especially like to thank the many dozens of brilliant teachers and authors who have shared their time and expertise with us for the past seventy-three years.

The Decision to Attend

by Jay Rehak

What matters when adulation becomes passé?

1

One-hundred-year-old renowned author Alice Bainbridge hated it when she was referred to as a "master storyteller." In her mind it always felt a little dishonest and a lot pretentious.

So when her caregiving grandson, Eddie, brought in the mail one cold Chicago January morning, and announced to her that she was to be honored in a month at the Midwest Writers Conference as a "master storyteller," Alice wasn't sure she would go.

"First of all, Eddie, I don't need any more awards. I mean, if they give me a plaque, what would I do with it? You'll just have to throw it out when I die. That's just a waste of a good piece of wood."

"Come on, Alice, it's something to look forward to," Eddie said.

"Second of all," Alice said, hearing Eddie all too well, "if I accept, who's to say I'll live until February? And if I don't, you'll have to spend a lot of time making phone calls and cancelling my appearance. A complete waste of your time. Let's skip it."

Eddie looked at his grandmother and decided he'd give her all the details before reminding her of the only reason she would want to go.

"The invitation says:

> Alice Bainbridge is being given a lifetime achievement award for all fifty-six of her novels and in honor of the 80th anniversary of the publication of her first known work, *Bedtime, A Comedy of Sorts*; and in special recognition of her newest novel, *Revelation, Remorse, and*

Restitution, which has earned the prestigious Book of the Year commendation.

Isn't that nice?"

"Yada, yada, blah, blah, blah, zis-coom-bah, la-de-da," Alice said, bored and exhausted by the idea. "Forget it, I'm too tired."

"We're going," Eddie said.

"Not interested," Alice said, closing her eyes, laying her head on the back of her wheelchair, and acting as if she were about to nod off to sleep or worse.

"Don't act like you're dying on me, Alice. I know you can hear me. You don't want to go pick up the award, fine. But, listen, a lot of storytellers will be there. A lot."

Alice opened her eyes and picked her head up off the back of her wheelchair. "You think they'll share?"

"Some will, some won't. Some might even bring copies with them. Of course, I don't know how good they'll be. But the whole room will be full of storytellers. Who else goes to a Writers' Conference?"

"Where's it being held?"

"Northwestern University in Evanston."

"Fine. If I make it to February, I'm in. Now let me get some sleep."

ε ε ε

When February rolled around, Alice was very much alive and very excited to attend, although she continued to complain to Eddie about having to waste time receiving the award up until the moment he wheeled her onto the stage in University Hall.

"If the emcee gets too long winded, I'm going to fake my death." Alice whispered to Eddie.

"Understood. Now be nice. These people are here to honor you."

"Well, I'm not here to be honored."

As Eddie wheeled her to the front of the stage, Alice was met by Jaime Ranier, a well-known mystery writer, who would be presenting Alice her award. As Jaime bent down to hug her, Alice shot a glance at Eddie.

Jamie began, "As you all know, we have come here today to honor a great novelist and playwright, a woman who, through her writing, has given the world many cathartic moments. Her power as an author has spanned decades. She has made us laugh. She has made us cry. She has made us care."

Alice looked at Eddie. She seemed ready to slump over in her chair. Eddie tried to signal her to be patient. Alice rolled her eyes as the emcee continued to drone on about her writing.

"From her first published work, we have felt Alice's pain and witnessed her resilience."

Alice closed her eyes, winced, and was suddenly motionless. For a moment, the audience thought she had nodded off or perhaps even...

But Alice was quite alive and quite awake. When she closed her eyes, she drifted back to being a little girl. She thought of the first book she had ever published. It was not *Bedtime, A Comedy of Sorts*. Not even close.

Alice was six when she published her first book, and she had called it *Alice's Silly Book*. She had created it out of colored construction paper. It was a small book, no more than eight pages, tied together on the edges by a bit of colored yarn. As she sat on stage, grimacing, Alice strained to think of a single line from it, but the memory of it all was too painful.

Alice shook off that memory and moved on to something more pleasant. She opened her eyes slowly, glowing at the thought of her high school days and her ambitions to someday write down something of consequence to her. The crowd misunderstood, convinced Alice was responding to Jaime Ranier's kind words. But Alice hadn't heard the flattery. She was too old for it.

Jaime Ranier was finally winding down. She picked up Alice's award and as she gently placed it on the old woman's lap, she said, "And so I present to you, Ms. Alice Bainbridge, Master Storyteller of the Year."

The crowd applauded and Alice nodded, signaling for the microphone. As Eddie held it in front of her mouth, the crowd became very still.

"Be nice," Eddie whispered.

Alice coughed, but her voice became stronger as she went on. "Thank you all for the nice plaque," Alice began, scanning the room before continuing. "I'm honored to be in a room full of writers and strivers. To be honest, when I was a little girl, I dreamed of a day like this." Alice paused to catch her breath.

People started to applaud, but Alice shook her head. "But as I got older, I realized how foolish that was. I realized the goal of writing was not to be recognized, but rather, to recognize ourselves in others. To realize that the stories we tell and the stories we hear are what unite us and help us better understand the human condition. To love, to fear, to want, to give, to receive and all feelings in between. From my first days as a writer, regardless how painful the memories, I came to understand who I am a little better, just as through reading and listening to others I understand a bit more of myself and the world I will soon be leaving."

She coughed again and seemed to choke up a bit, her eyes filling with tears. Many in the audience shifted in their seats. Alice realized this and recovered, "I'm almost done. Just one more thing. I'm going to have my grandson wheel me over to that table." She shakily pointed her right index finger towards her left. "If anyone would like to speak to me, I'd appreciate it. As you can tell, I'm not much of a talker, but I do know how to listen. In fact, when I'm dead, which can't be too far down the road, I'd much prefer to be remembered not as a Master Storyteller, but as a Master Story Listener. So if anyone wants to stop by and tell me a story, maybe some seminal event you've had or maybe something you've just made up, I'd love it. Because listening to good stories is pretty much what's keeping me alive. So please, tell me a story. That's my reason for being here. Thank you again."

With that, the crowd burst into applause. A number of people exited to the adjacent exhibit hall, where vendors were handing out pens and other swag.

As Eddie brought Alice over to the table, many people lined up to speak to her. Some came to congratulate her and tell her how much they enjoyed her books. Alice was polite but short with them. Her time and energy was limited and she was looking to be inspired, not praised. After the third person had

4

congratulated her, Alice began yawning. Eddie bent down and asked her if she wanted to go home. Alice whispered to him, "At this point I'm thinking about drifting off further than that."

"Stop it," Eddie said playfully.

"All right then, I'm not leaving until I hear a good story, Eddie. But if I don't hear one soon, I'm shuffling off this mortal coil!"

Eddie shook his head at his grandmother then looked at the people in line. None of them knew it, but it was up to at least one of them to keep her alive.

— JAY C. REHAK —————————————

...created the storyline for *A Reason to Be Here*. He is the co-author of numerous crowd-source novels including *30 Days to Empathy*, the world's first high school class-sourced novel. His comedic plays have been produced around the world. His *10 Short Plays You Need to Read Before You Die* is available on Amazon, or by visiting www.sidelineinkpublishing. com. Jay is currently writing *Sideline & Company*, the third novel in his middle grade *Sideline* series. He invites everyone to visit his website: www.laughsaver.com and record a bit of their laughter.

The Haircut

by Elizabeth DeSchryver

A girl's rebellion triggers revelations from her
stern grandmother.

2

"Yvonne. Yvonne Clarkson," the woman said, extending her hand. Alice took it in both of hers. "You're very different from my grandmamma," Yvonne said. "But there's something about your writing that reminds me of her."

"Is that a good thing?"

"Oh yes. We became very close. Because of a haircut, of all things."

"Tell me." Alice settled into her chair.

Yvonne began.

& & &

My grandmamma…well, back when I was a kid, I saw her as a pointy-chinned force of propriety, with a stare that could make your stomach fold in on itself. In spite of forty years in Chicago, she still spoke with a distinct French accent that made her sound elegant and disapproving at the same time. One did not put one's elbows on the table in her presence. Or speak until spoken to.

She came to Sunday dinner at least once a month. I never knew what she really thought of us, her grandchildren. She believed my mother had married beneath her. She never said a word about my parent's divorce, but there was always a thin smile as she took my father's place at the head of the table.

One particular Sunday, a small battle was fought. Every year, in June, my mother chopped our hair into short pixie cuts—the same cut for Madeline, Tommy, and me. I hated it. Passionately. I wanted long, flowing hair, like all the other girls in third grade. I wanted it to curl around my shoulders, hide my eyes when I sneaked glances at boys. But most of all, I hated the teasing. "Hey, melon-head," Dickie Myers would call. "You tryin' ta be a boy?"

That year, I refused to have my hair cut with a fiery desperation that shocked both my mother and me. My mother argued, cajoled, and finally lost patience.

"Yvonne Marie, I don't have time for this," she said. "Your grandmother—"

"No!" I ran out of the room, her voice chasing after me.

"This isn't over, young lady!"

I kept running. I hid in the blackberry bushes behind the garage. No one came there, because of the prickers and the wasps. But if you sat really still, neither one would bother you.

Hours later, Madeline found me there. "Mom said to come and get cleaned up," she said, shaking her newly cut hair. "Grandmamma will be here in half an hour. Don't worry, she doesn't have time to cut your hair now."

I didn't answer. I just brushed off the dirt as best I could and snuck back in the house to change. Grandmamma did not approve of wearing shorts at dinner.

I slipped into the dining room last, giving my grandmother the obligatory peck on the cheek. After grace, her gray eyes fixed on me. "My, what long hair you have, my dear."

"She refused to have her hair cut this afternoon," my mother replied. "She suddenly hated the idea."

"And you allowed this rebellion?"

"For now."

Grandmamma looked at me. Her eyes narrowed. "Obedience in a child is a great virtue," she said. "Have you forgotten, Yvonne?"

"No, ma'am."

"Will you permit your mother to cut your hair?"

"I really don't want her to, ma'am."

"And what is your reason for this, this resistance?"

"I don't want to look like a boy." I stared down at my plate. "Kids make fun of me."

"I see." It was Grandmamma's most ominous phrase.

Silence fell, except for the clink of silverware chiming in muted discord. No one wanted to draw attention when Grandmamma was in this mood.

Dinner crawled to an end. Grandmamma rose from the table. "Yvonne, come with me. Charlotte, where are the scissors?"

"Mother, you don't have to—"

"I insist."

I followed Grandmamma upstairs to my mother's room, which was where the butchery would take place. She stood me in front of the mirror.

"Look in the mirror, child. What do you see?"

I looked. I didn't dare give a smart-aleck answer. "A girl," I said slowly. "A girl with freckles and a round nose and gray eyes and nice hair."

"What else?"

"I don't know what you mean."

Grandmamma sighed. "How old are you, Yvonne?"

"Eight. And three quarters."

"Too young," she said, almost to herself. "Well, Yvonne eight-and-three-quarters, why does this haircut matter so much to you?"

"Because I want to feel pretty," I said. I didn't think she'd like that answer, but it was the truth.

"And that is important?"

"Some," I admitted. "Mostly, I just want to like how I look. And not have kids make fun of me."

Grandmamma sighed again. "Lay this sheet on the floor, and stand on it." I did as I was told, and stood ramrod straight, fists clenched at my sides. I closed my eyes.

Snip, snip.

I winced.

Snip snip snip. The scissors slid around my head like a creature of the night. Snip, snip. "I think that will do."

I opened my eyes. There in the mirror was a freckled face, a snub nose— and shoulder-length hair. Beautiful, trim, shoulder-length hair, barely an inch shorter than it had been ten minutes ago. I tossed my head and felt the tips of my hair like the swirl of a paint brush. I laughed, joy and relief bubbling up inside me. Then I met Grandmamma's eyes in the mirror.

"Someday you will learn," she said quietly, "that the flapping laughter of others does not matter. That appearances do not matter. But," she said more firmly, "self-confidence can make all the difference. Liking yourself can matter even more." She brushed a wisp of hair off my shoulder. "So this is my gift to you, from one who remembers what it was like to be young and ridiculed."

I opened my mouth to say thank you, but instead, a question came out. "Grandmamma?"

"Yes?"

"What happened to you? Did someone make fun of you, too?"

She paused, and then shook her head. "You are too young," she said again. "But someday, I will tell you. Now clean all this up before you come downstairs."

Something changed that night, between my grandmother and me. Maybe she sensed a kindred spirit. Maybe I was less afraid of her, knowing she could bend a little. But bit by bit, we became friends.

I came away with something else, though, something I didn't realize until much later. I think, deep down, that it was my first realization that adults had hidden stories. I mean, I knew things had happened to them before I met them, the way you know the world is round without seeing for yourself. But from then on, I understood that I was surrounded by hidden stories, stories waiting to be heard, experiences that made people behave in ways you'd never expect. I became fascinated by them. I think that was the day I became a writer. In my heart, at least.

 ፚ ፚ ፚ

Yvonne's glance returned to Alice, pulling away from that long-ago moment. "And did your grandmother ever tell you her story?" Alice asked.

"Years later," Yvonne admitted.

"Tell me."

Yvonne hesitated, glancing at the line of people snaking behind her. "Perhaps I should let someone else take a turn."

"Oh, no, you're not getting away with that," Alice said. "Now, talk."

Yvonne met her gaze, but with an odd hint of sadness in her eyes. "My grandmamma," Yvonne began, "lived in France during World War II. She was lovely, unmarried, and very Aryan-looking, all of which brought her to the uncomfortable attention of the German officers. Some offered crude jokes. Others were more menacing. She realized that eventually she would have to choose one as a protector."

"I understand," Alice said.

"Some approached her with kindness instead of slurs, gave her extra food or coal. So she picked the highest ranking one, a hauptmann—a captain, that is—and became his mistress. She tried to hide the liaison. But people knew. They avoided her, or spat after she walked past.

"Soon her...involvement...came to the attention of the Resistance. But instead of castigating her, they wanted to use her. Have her tease information out of her lover. Get him to take her places they couldn't go. She said she would try." Yvonne paused. "She didn't want to. It was dangerous. But it was just as dangerous to say no."

"Between a rock and a hard place," Alice commented, nodding.

"But the request changed her," Yvonne said. "It helped her distance herself from the services she was providing, to feel that she could be sacrificing herself for more than just staying alive. So she began collecting tidbits of information, expressing an interest in his work. She never knew if it did any good," Yvonne admitted. "No matter what she told her Resistance contact, he would sneer and say, 'Is that all?' But it became as necessary for her as breathing."

"She was keeping her soul alive," Alice said.

Yvonne nodded. "When the war ended, the French took revenge on the women who had slept with the Germans. "*Collaboration horizontale,* they called it. They dragged them out of their homes, forced them to their knees, and shaved their heads. Then they paraded them through the streets. My grandmamma was one of them."

"But her work for the Resistance?"

"Might have spared her, if the crowd had known. But she had no proof. And no one came forward to speak for her."

"Maybe they were all dead."

"No." Yvonne's voice had a bitter edge. "When they were finished with her, she looked up and saw him, her Resistance contact, standing there in the crowd. Just watching."

Alice opened her mouth to speak, but then just shook her head.

"She staggered to her feet, grabbing a hank of her hair from the gravel. She lunged at him. 'You knew!' she cried out, shaking the hair in his face. 'You knew I was helping the Resistance!' The crowd murmured, waiting for him to deny it.

"He just glared at her. 'You are still a whore,' he finally said. And walked away. No one bothered Grandmamma after that." Yvonne smiled grimly. "And, in that town at least, no more heads were shaved."

"How old was she, when all this happened?" Alice asked.

"Nineteen."

"Oh, dear God," Alice breathed. "I can see why she didn't tell you all this when you were eight."

"It wasn't until I was working on my PhD that she began telling me stories of the war. I guess she thought I could handle it by then."

"Um, before this turns into another story..." Eddie started.

"I know, I know, people are waiting," Alice said with a dismissive flap of her hand.

"Thank you for being so generous with your time," Yvonne said.

"Thank you for making it worth my time," Alice said. "And for the record..."

"Yes?"

"I think you have *lovely* hair."

Yvonne laughed. "Thank you." She walked away with a small wave, exiting to the exhibition hall.

ELIZABETH DESCHRYVER

...is a retired methodologist who is glad finally to be doing something that people recognize. She has been writing since childhood, and now has no excuse not to get serious about it. She is a playwright and poet, and has been a member of OCWW for several years.

I've Got Your Number

by Adrianne Hayward

Nore faces hard choices after falling in love
with a married man.

3

As yet another gushy well-wisher finally left the table, a tall, dark woman wearing wire-framed glasses and a purple beret stepped up to greet Alice. The woman spared a tight-lipped, half smile before leaning down and whispering, "I've never told anyone this story."

Alice's azure eyes brightened in anticipation. "Tell me your name, dear."

"I'm Lenore Holloway, Ms. Bainbridge, but everyone calls me Nore."

"Well, it's a pleasure to meet you, Nore. Please call me Alice."

"After reading so many of your books, I feel like I know you," Nore said, as she seated herself at Alice's table. "Your words consistently comfort and inspire me. What you said today—about writing helping you better understand yourself and the world—is true. I know because of the insight I gain from reading your books.

"When Jaime Ranier said your stories are cathartic, I remembered reading *Bedtime: A Comedy of Sorts* for the first time. Reading about Bella's struggles and how she persevered helped me cope. It's as if you created that character especially for me, and I read it just when I needed it most—December 1972, my first Christmas away from home and family.

"I always thought, if given a chance, I'd like to say or do something to let you know what an inspiration you are. So, when you asked for a story..."

Alice nodded encouragingly and sat up straighter in her wheelchair. Nore took a deep, fortifying breath and launched into her tale:

ε ε ε

I was 22 when I graduated from Northwestern and moved to Colorado—a thousand miles away from my home on Chicago's South Side—to start my career as a *Denver Post* reporter.

In no time, I was settling into the first apartment I'd ever lived in alone—no parents, no roommates—and this cute guy, Carl, was installing my telephone.

As he was leaving, he asked, "Would you mind if I give you call? I already have your number."

He smiled; I laughed. I was flattered, so I said okay. Then I held out a notepad and pen and asked for his phone number.

"You must be one of those women's libbers," he said, while scribbling down his number.

"I wish! I believe in equal rights for women, but I'm still my mother's daughter. She says it's un-ladylike to telephone men; in her opinion, anyone who does is a hussy. We both got a good laugh out of that."

I appreciated the way Carl accommodated my 4 p.m. to midnight work shift at the *Post* by calling on my days off. After a few phone chats, he was still flattering me and I was still laughing at his witticisms, so I said yes when he asked me to go out with him. Since we had no mutual friends, I wanted our first date to be in a public place, so we met at beautiful Estes Park.

It's hard to imagine a more gorgeous amusement park setting. The mountains, the trees, the gardens—everything was sunny, lush and green—like walking through a picture postcard!

We spent the whole day there, talking, laughing, and stuffing ourselves with ice cream and cotton candy. We rode the most dangerous rollercoasters before winding down with rides and stolen kisses on the park's vintage merry-go-round. That's when I started falling in love.

This all happened in July. In early August, my mother called and announced she was flying out for a visit at the end of September. I told her all about Carl and how anxious I was for them to meet. I was eager to share the good news, so I searched my purse for Carl's number. As I dialed, I realized it was my first time calling him. The phone rang once before I heard a child's voice say, "Hi."

"Oh, so sorry," I said. "I must have the wrong number. I was trying to reach Carl Ewing."

"Daddy's not home," she said, and I heard a woman's chiding voice saying, "Carla, how many times have I told you to let me know, right away, whenever the phone rings? Who's on the line?"

I immediately ended the call. I wish that was the end of my story.

I did the right thing—at first. My shock, rage and hurt came out in a torrent of tears, threats, and an endless stream of expletives–none deleted. When he rang my doorbell a week later, I gave him more of the same.

I started going out with a marketing guy I knew from the Press Club, but that ended after he stood me up one Saturday night. I was so angry and frustrated, I stomped my feet and yelled, "Nobody in this whole damn city loves me." I was homesick, too; I missed my Chicago family and friends.

The loneliness festered.

When Carl stopped by over the Labor Day weekend, wearing a sad smile and carrying a dozen pink roses, I surrendered.

Carl was with me when I picked up my mother from the airport. He took us out to a pricey seafood restaurant, followed by drinks at an intimate little jazz club where Ahmad Jamal (Mom's favorite) was performing. Carl went all out to show us a good time, but it was obvious my mother didn't like him.

"Where is he heading in life, Lenore? What can he afford to do for you that you can't afford to do for yourself?'

A week later, I found myself on an examination table at the Planned Parenthood center on Race Street, babbling, non-stop, about being an enlightened, independent woman, known for being smart, reliable and level-headed.

I can't be pregnant! It's not like me to be so unbelievably irresponsible. All the effort I put into becoming the first person in my family to graduate college. My parents will be so disappointed–hell, I'm disappointed! I'll have to quit my job and go home. What kind of example will that set? When did I lose my mind?

Remember, this was 1972, shortly before Roe v. Wade took effect. Only four states allowed legal abortion. Because of my measly $100-a-week salary, I asked for financial help and, by November, Planned Parenthood had arranged an appointment with a reputable physician and a round-trip flight to Seattle.

Can you believe I fully expected to be able to baptize my aborted baby? When I asked to see the fetus, the doctor had to repeat himself because his response didn't register with me right away.

He said, "There's nothing left to see, let alone pray over."

I had anticipated the guilt. The grief took me by surprise.

Another month passed before I mustered enough courage to tell Carl about Seattle. Seeing the bullet-dodging expression of relief wash over his face irked me. He was so appreciative, offering to help pay for the abortion and asking how much it cost.

"Thirty pieces of silver," I whispered, but I knew he couldn't hear me. When he left that night, I knew he was gone for good.

I sat on the sofa with my chin resting on my knees and my arms circling my legs, rocking and crying until the sun came up—but I never shed a single tear for Carl.

ε ε ε

Alice placed a comforting hand on Nore's shoulder and softly asked, "Did you ever hear from Carl again?"

"Sort of, about a year later. It was one day before I left Denver for a new job in Chicago. He asked me what I'd say if he told me his wife had left him."

"I said, 'I'd say that's too bad, because everybody needs somebody.' I hung up before he could say anything else.

"Isn't it strange, Alice, that some of the most life-altering decisions we make—choosing a college, selecting a major, accepting the right first job, deciding where to live, getting married, starting a family—are made when we're so young, naïve, and unprepared? That's why Bella, and the other feisty heroines you create, are so important. They inspire us to learn from past mistakes and keep moving forward.

Alice nodded as Nore walked away, seemingly unburdened, if only temporarily, by telling her story.

— ADRIANNE HAYWARD

...was a newspaper reporter before embarking on a successful career in corporate communications and cause-related marketing. As a retiree, she turned to writing fiction, and is working on a first novel.

The Last Word

by Hollie Smurthwaite

Lania struggles to accept her past.

4

Lania studied the backs of the heads in front of her, wondering why she was standing in a line to bitch out a hundred-year-old woman. That had to be a sin. And what did she expect Alice to do, re-write everything she'd ever written? Kill all the happy endings and hope? All the same...*Revelation, Remorse, and Restitution*? Lania's revelation was that there was no remorse or restitution out there.

She should just go. But then the line moved forward one, which seemed like a sign. Lania unclenched her hand from her purse and breathed into her diaphragm. Living a secret destroys. Of course, opening up a secret didn't necessarily mean you told everyone. Still, if she had to read one more uplifting, silver-lining, whatever-doesn't-kill-you-makes-you-stronger book, she was going to implode.

Nothing she did or said ever changed anything. Yet, every time she shifted her weight to duck out of the line, her feet wouldn't move. Alice had to know that not everyone had a redeeming ending. She thought about what she'd say, how she could condense what had happened to her into something coherent. The memories surged forward. The smell of stale sweat and beer choked her. Trapped. Trapped. Too much.

Breathe. Another breath, deep, into the diaphragm. Hold and hold. Exhale, slow, steady, letting all the pain and anger flow out. Again. Again.

And then Alice was before her, sitting in a wheelchair, wearing that flowery dress, her blue eyes more alive than Lania's had been for years. "Lania Patire," she said, her voice a croak.

Lania took the woman's frail hand, knuckles swollen, the skin papery and dry, yet somehow soft. Alice's humanity was a confusing balm to her molten anger. She needed that anger. It was all she had. The attention of Alice and her companion amassed with the press of people lined up behind them. They waited for her to say something. Wanting their own turns. But Lania couldn't find the right words. Any words.

"I said no." It was no more than a whisper. Lania could see the woman hadn't heard her.

She sat down at the table in front of Alice, putting their eyes level. She couldn't whisper or sob if she wanted Alice to hear her, to understand any of it. As if what had happened to her was even understandable. "I said no."

Alice put her hand over Lania's. Lania put her hand on top of that one, and Alice topped the pile with her other hand, like stacks of pancakes.

"He was handsome and charming and..." Lania swallowed. "I was so flattered when he asked me out. We'd talked a few times, and he remembered everything I told him—little, stupid things about my classes and my family. His folks were from Glenview and mine were from Waukegan, which aren't all that close, but there was some overlap in teams we'd played in high school. I played tennis and he played basketball."

Lania shook her head. Those details weren't important, and there was a line behind her.

"We went out twice. But then..." She swallowed and tried to breathe. "He wanted to see my apartment. And I wanted him to come up." Lania hardened her voice. "I hadn't decided yet if I was going to sleep with him. It seemed early, but he was gorgeous, and I wanted him to like me. But he changed. As soon as the door was closed and locked, he became a different person."

"You're safe now," Alice said.

Lania shook her head. Nobody was safe. "He was aggressive and strong. I couldn't stop him."

Alice turned to look up at her assistant. "Eddie, could you please get Lania a beverage?"

Lania had forgotten about the balding man who shared Alice's eyes, she'd been so captivated by Alice. He looked glad to step away, which twisted her insides. Maybe he judged her, or maybe he was just uncomfortable. He wasn't gone long.

"Thanks," she said to Eddie, who smelled vaguely of vanilla. She took a tentative sip of water before turning her attention back to Alice.

Lowering her voice, unwilling to share her story with a man just yet, if she could help it, Lania said, "I said no. And I said it pretty much non-stop, but he just ignored me." She learned the meaning of dead eyes that night. He'd looked through her, focusing on nothing. Like a doll, his face held no expression. No lust or anger or guilt.

Lania cleared her throat. "I struggled, but it didn't do any good. He..."
She couldn't say it.

"Raped you," Alice finished, her voice softer than her hands.

The story couldn't be stopped now. "He never hit me, so all I had were a few bruises on my wrists and thighs." She wanted to lower her voice more, but Alice was one hundred years old, and there was no reason to feel shame.

"They did a rape kit, but never processed it. The State's Attorney didn't think the case was strong enough. He-said, she-said and all that." She bit her lip. "He didn't get kicked out of school either. The university didn't care. And nobody believed me because he didn't need to rape anyone to get sex. Even most of my friends thought that maybe I mistook passion for rape or, even worse, that I sort of fooled myself afterwards because I felt guilty for being a slut."

"That's not right," Alice said.

"I talked about almost nothing else for a long time, but people started mocking me for it. Even the few friends who believed me thought I should have moved on after a few months. But how could I? How could I move on when my entire life was ruined and..." She swallowed. "His life didn't change at all. He was walking around whole and happy while my life was all con-fuckulated. I can't let it go. Over five years later and I can't forget." Like a dam breaking, words crashed and flowed everywhere. "But I stopped talking about

23

it, because nobody wanted to hear it. I tried to pretend that I was normal, that I had thoughts and feelings like everyone else. "For years, I kept it a secret, thinking I was protecting myself, but it didn't make it any better. And then, when I thought I couldn't take living another day, I called the hotline." Lania swiped at her wet face. "The woman I talked to calmed me down and gave me a therapy referral."

"Did it help?"

Bitterness clung to Lania. "Sure. Except it doesn't change what happened. I stalked him on Instagram. He's married and he has a kid and a Jeep Grand Cherokee and he's so fucking happy and smug and living the kind of life that he has no fucking right to live. He took everything from me. He has no remorse whatsoever. Where is my goddamned *restitution*, Alice?"

Lania collapsed into herself, her face in her hands. Alice put her weathered hand on Lania's shoulder, not saying anything. Eventually, Lania felt the broken pieces of herself trying to find their way to one another again. Eddie handed her a tissue, which she took without looking at him. She didn't want to see the spectacle she'd become reflected on his face. On anyone's face.

"I started writing articles for women's magazines, some print and some online. It helps with the anger." Lania looked up at Alice and half smiled. "Not all of it, obviously, but I hope that by talking about sexual assault and discrimination and rape culture that maybe I can help change our world."

Alice nodded. "Just remember, healing is a choice."

"What?"

"Nothing can undo what happened to you, but you don't have to let it define you." Alice leaned forward, her eyes snapping with intensity.

"Hasn't it already?"

Alice smiled, looking suddenly wise and powerful, like the Dali Lama and the Earth Mother combined. "We continually define ourselves every moment we're alive."

It sounded like truth.

"Besides," Alice said. "You don't want to let that bastard have the last word."

Lania spluttered a laugh. "Did you just say 'bastard?'"

24

Alice smiled. "I thought motherfucker might be too shocking."

Hearing a hundred-year-old woman say "motherfucker" reminded Lania that life was full of the unexpected—and it wasn't always a bad thing. "I think motherfucker is about right, Alice."

She giggled; then they both laughed. "Thank you for that."

Alice gave her hand one last pat. "You'll be all right."

Lania still wasn't sure, but the woman had lived to be a hundred years old. And maybe it wasn't Alice's works that needed a re-write. Maybe it was Lania.

HOLLIE SMURTHWAITE

...has been a member of OCWW since 2016. Past professions have included: checkout clerk, administrative assistant, violence prevention speaker, and belly dancer. She has numerous prospective novels in various states of undress. Currently, she lives in Chicago with her husband, son, and too few pets. www.holliesmurthwaite.com.

Killing Teddy

by Renee James

A transgender child goes swimming with a bully.

5

While she waited in line, a tall, broad-shouldered woman with a quiet smile and a brisk air looked up from scribbling in her notebook to scan the faces of the people around her. She chatted with the woman in front of her, but it was a gray-haired couple about six heads behind her that drew her attention. They were staring at her, eyes rounded, tongues wagging. They didn't point, but their focus was obviously on the tall woman.

The tall woman smiled at the couple, scribbled in her notebook, looked up at them again, and scribbled again, and smiled at them again.

When she reached the front of the line, the woman put away her pen and notepad and extended her hand. Alice accepted the woman's handshake.

"Hi, what's your na—" Alice began, politely.

"My name isn't important," said the woman. "I'm not important, either, but I have a story that could have come right out of *Revelation, Remorse, and Restitution*, so you might find it amusing."

Alice smiled and nodded for the woman to go ahead.

ც ც ც

Mel lived in a valley in central Washington state, a semi-arid, rural place with dirt roads and sagebrush hills and long walks to the nearest neighbor's house. The only green things were apple orchards, and they were green only because snow-melt was channeled down from the mountains in rivers and irrigation canals for the specific purpose of making the orchards bloom.

Mel was a seven-year-old boy with reddish blonde hair and a nice smile, but his parents worried about him because he preferred to play with his sister's dolls and wear her clothes instead of doing boy things. His parents were kind, so they didn't punish him for being effeminate, but they encouraged him to do boy things whenever they could.

Which was how it came to pass that Mel found himself on the banks of an irrigation canal one August afternoon. He was wearing boy swimming trunks and he was supposed to be playing with Agnes Whipple's grandson, Teddy. For Mel, there were several things wrong with the scenario right from the start. For one, the water in the canals was snow melt, so even in August, it was cold enough to turn your lips blue in a few minutes.

For two, Agnes was a bit of a dim bulb who thought Teddy was a sweet boy. She missed a lot of the reality taking place around her.

For three, Teddy was a dull, nasty boy with a glowering countenance and a mean streak so obvious, Mel could almost taste it when they were introduced.

Agnes sat on a picnic blanket and opened a book, encouraging the boys to play nicely. Mel looked dubiously at Teddy, but resolved to try his best to get along with him. Teddy had a bag of floating toys, including an elaborate model of a Navy destroyer. Mel unrolled his towel and took out a plastic boat he'd brought along. It was a cheap toy, a depiction of a cabin cruiser that had been stuffed in his Christmas stocking last winter. It was a strange present for a kid who lived in the desert. They didn't even have a bathtub. The ditch in front of their house only carried water for a few weeks in the spring. Mel had never seen a lake or a swimming pool. The irrigation canals were the only bodies of water nearby and that water was so cold, no sane person swam in them. Which said a lot about Teddy.

They started in shallow water, floating their own boats. They worked their way into deeper water, waist high, Teddy leading the way, seemingly impervious to the cold. Mel's teeth chattered and his pale skin erupted in goose bumps.

"Are you cold?" Teddy asked. Except he didn't ask. It was more of a taunt.

"Yes." Mel tried not to say it like a girl, because he knew how offended people got when he did that, but he was too cold to be subtle.

"Are you a girl?" Teddy asked.

"No," said Mel. "I'm a boy, but I like girl things."

He turned away from Teddy, trying to cut off the conversation, knowing where it was headed, but Teddy was persistent. "Watch this," Teddy said. He filled his boat with water and let it sink to the bottom of the canal, then dove in head-first to retrieve it, splashing Mel with an Arctic shower in the process. Teddy stood in chest-deep water, brandishing his boat triumphantly. "Got it!" he yelled.

Mel shivered and watched.

"You're kind of a sissy, aren't you." It wasn't a question. Teddy said it with a trace of contempt in his voice. "Come on, you dive now."

Mel was horrified at the thought. He glanced from Teddy to Agnes, hoping for help, but Agnes had dozed off in the warm August sun. "No," said Mel. "It's too cold."

"Come on, don't be a sissy," said Teddy, splashing toward Mel now, an evil smile on his face.

"No," Mel said, turning away from him. Teddy smiled wider and started slapping the water to pelt Mel in spray. "Come on, sissy, let's have a water fight."

Mel hurried out of the canal and shivered on the bank.

"Play nice, you two," Agnes called from her towel, still half asleep.

"It's too cold," said Mel, and he started to towel himself off. He'd catch hell for going home so soon, but he didn't care. Teddy was a toad and his grandmother was an idiot and anyone stupid enough play in snow melt deserved to die of pneumonia.

"Okay, come on, Mel," Teddy called from the water. "I'll be good. Let's sail the boats."

After more cajoling, and against his better judgment, Mel waded back into the water. They floated their boats back and forth, Mel upstream of Teddy, releasing them to float to him in the current, Teddy swimming them back, seizing the opportunity to splash Mel in icy water and watch him flinch like a girl and shiver.

Teddy got bored with the game. "Let's dive for the boats," he said. Mel objected, but Teddy insisted it would be fun. Mel could sink them, then he'd retrieve them. Mel shrugged and went along with the game, figuring it was the best he was going to do until he could go home.

It was mildly amusing. Mel would submerge a boat in the water and cast it adrift in the current. Teddy would wait for it to pass him, then dive like Tarzan and splash like an elephant and pluck the vessel from the water. His antics were mildly entertaining, but best of all, he was far enough away that Mel didn't get splashed.

It couldn't last, of course, and after five minutes or so, Teddy dove after Mel's cheap plastic cabin cruiser. This time, instead of standing up and waving the boat in the air, he stood and yelled, "I can't find it. I'll try again."

Teddy made three dives into the water, each time coming up empty-handed, pretending to be apologetic and distraught. Mel watched with disgust. The thing about the canals was, they were concrete lined and the water was as clear as glass and you could see things twenty feet away in the water. Mel could easily see the boat under Teddy's foot.

"I still can't find it," Teddy called.

Mel shrugged and started to get out of the water. Teddy called for him to help look for the boat.

"Look under your foot," Mel said.

"It's not there," Teddy replied. Mel studied his ugly toad face, the cruel eyes, the smirking mouth. He shrugged and waded out of the canal.

"If I find it, can I keep it?" called Teddy.

"If you find it you can shove it up your ass," said Mel. He had been learning the colorful language of the farmworkers' kids who traveled through the valley for the harvests.

Mel's cursing woke Agnes from her nap. "Mel Gray, where did you learn to talk like that? I'm going to tell your parents!"

Mel barely acknowledged the adult. He walked to his towel, pulled his pants on over his trunks, slid on his shoes, and picked up everything else. He headed down the hill toward home, a mile away through the high-desert brush.

"You apologize to poor Teddy right now," Agnes yelled. "He's been looking forward to this all week!"

Mel stopped, turned, and waved to Teddy. "Sorry, Teddy," he said. He started to leave again, but Agnes was standing now, calling to him.

"Why are you leaving?" asked Agnes.

Mel thought of all the things he could say at that moment. *Because Teddy doesn't like sissies. Because Teddy is a big mean snot. Because I don't need to be bullied by a moron.* But he didn't say any of them.

"Because I need to go home and kill Teddy," he said. And Mel skipped happily home through the short dry grasses and around the spreading sagebrush stands, humming happily and keeping an eye out for rattlesnakes. When he got home, he pulled out the spiral notebook and the number-two pencil that had been in his Christmas stocking along with the cheap plastic boat, and he wrote a story about Teddy.

ε ε ε

"It took forever to write, even though the story was only three sentences long," the woman told Alice. "In the first sentence, they met. In the second sentence, Teddy got the boat. And in the third sentence Teddy got a cramp and drowned. I've been making life hell for bullies in my stories ever since."

Alice wasn't sure how to react. She raised her eyebrows in confusion.

"Empowerment," said the woman with the quiet smile. She said the word as though it explained everything. "That's why I write. My stories make me the mistress of my own worlds."

The tall woman paused and looked back at the angry couple in the crowd. She mouthed the words, "Thank you," to them, and then turned back to Alice.

"As a matter of fact," she said to Alice, "I have to hurry home to bury a couple of people I met today."

— RENEE JAMES —

...is a confessed English major and an out transgender author. After a career in magazines, she has written four up-market thrillers and a literary adventure novel. She currently has two novels in progress and has volunteered as co-director of OCWW programming since 2016.

The Healer

by Tonya Coats

Racial put-downs help an African-American
woman accept her destiny.

"Alice, you look tired. Are you ready to go?" Eddie leaned down and whispered into Alice's ear. "I'm sure everyone would understand."

"Oh, no, no, Eddie. Look at that line. I can't leave now after I promised them to listen." She swatted him away as she focused on the next person waiting to pay tribute. She smiled eagerly and signaled the woman over. The woman, of average height, had shiny milk chocolate skin and eyes the exact color of her skin. The uniformity was striking.

"Well, this one certainly looks like she will be interesting to talk to," Alice said as Eddie walked away.

Camille Tolliver wore a brightly colored and billowing outfit. She pulled her skirts around her and sat down at the table in front of Alice and gingerly wrapped both of her hands around Alice's free hand. Alice shivered a bit and looked down at their entwined fingers. She tried to pull her hand away but Camille held them firm. She looked back up at the woman, blue eyes to brown eyes, questioning.

"Your hands are so warm. I feel like you just shocked me," Alice said with wonder.

"Miss Bainbridge," Camille began, "you surely won't remember me, but we met almost thirty years ago and you helped me so much…"

"Thirty years ago, you must have been a child dear," Alice cut in. "Are you even forty? What's your name? Where did we meet? How did I help you?" She fired off her questions in rapid succession, typical old lady style.

Camille chuckled and answered patiently, "I'm Camille, Camille Tolliver. I have been around for forty-seven years. When I was a freshman at Stanford

University I wanted to be a writer. I was smart and confident. But my first English class wasn't going very well. You see, I had attended a small Lutheran high school in the inner city of Chicago. I never struggled in my English classes there, but in the first quarter of college I was struggling to even get a 'C' in the class. I met you and you helped me. If it hadn't been for you, I might have tried to drop out and gone back to Chicago."

"Ah yes. Stanford. I remember. I had such a warm welcome there," Alice said and she stacked her free hand on top of Camille's, pulled her in closer, and peered deep into her eyes searching for recognition. "I had expected to spend so much more time with the faculty and was so surprised at how much contact I had with the students. I felt so inspired during my quarter there. I must have gotten inspiration for at least three of my novels." She seemed to fall into a trance, lost in the memories.

Camille gave a slight shake of their entwined hands that startled Alice and brought her back. "Oh, oh, I think I was far away wasn't I?" Alice blushed a little.

"No worries." Camille smiled.

"So you say I inspired you? How so? We met? Honestly…I'm so sorry…This old brain…I really don't remember you. It was so long ago you know. But I'd like to. Perhaps you can jog my memory."

"You sat in my literature class and we were discussing the presence of phallic symbols, but because I had gone to an inner city Lutheran school…"

"You had no idea what they were talking about," Alice said, finishing Camille's thought. "I remember."

"Everyone was laughing at me," Camille said, "but I didn't know. Discussing sexuality was taboo at my school. But my classmates assumed because I was African-American and from Chicago that my education wasn't up to par."

"Oh, I remember," Alice said. "And the Professor, Professor Loesser, I remember her. She was just as bad as the students. Didn't she ask if you had ever taken an English class?"

"Yes she did. She rolled her eyes at me and muttered something about how she didn't know how I got in, and that this was affirmative action at its worse. That's when you got up and started yelling at all of them, particularly at Professor Loesser. You said, 'What kind of morons do they let teach in this school?' But for me the damage was done. I left the class in tears."

"You had such good ideas and potential. So are you a writer? Would I have seen any of your work?"

"No. I ended up getting out of the English department."

"Oh, no. That's too bad," Alice lamented. "So what do you do?"

"Well, I'm a doctor, a healer."

"Oh. A healer you say." Alice was incredulous but then looked down at their hands. "Is that what I feel? I mean, is that why your hands feel so soothing to me?"

"I know it seems weird. I don't usually tell people I'm a healer. Being a doctor is enough."

"But you are telling me, why?"

"I wanted to be a writer, still do, but my family sent me away to become a doctor. After that incident in the literature class I thought it was a sign and I shouldn't go against my destiny and the plans my family had for me."

"I see."

"I come from a long lineage of healers. My family lore is that when we were free in Africa, we were part of a family of healers, medicine men, and root women. My first slave ancestor in America, my five-times great-grandfather, Papa Cudjo, was a medicine man who was brought here in the late 1700s. Because of our history of healers, our lineage was better preserved than most and since we had to pass down our practices we also kept better track of our lineage."

"That's fascinating."

"Yes, so after Papa Cudjo, my four-times, three-times, and two-times great-grandmothers were all known as wet nurses and root women throughout their enslavements. They were valuable on the plantation as healers to the slaves and sometimes the master's family. So their family unit was kept intact instead of being sold apart as often happened to the enslaved. My great-grandmother who was the first one to be born after the emancipation was a midwife and made a great living for our family. Her daughter was a registered mid-wife and my mother is still working as a nurse. But everyone always said we have healing hands. It's true. I know I feel my patient's energy and sometimes I can push my energy into them."

"Is that the story you want to write?" Alice encouraged.

"I think so. I've actually started it."

"Then finish it. I know you can and it will be great. I only hope I'll still be around to read the finished project."

Camille squeezed Alice's hand a little more firmly and once again Alice shook. But this time she didn't pull her hand away.

"Thanks for your encouragement, then and now. I think you'll be around to read it. I'll finish it as fast as I can. I look forward to seeing you here next year." Then Camille got up, kissed Alice on her downy soft crown, turned and disappeared into the crowd.

— DR. TONYA COATS

...is a native Chicagoan. She is currently on an indefinite leave from medicine to pursue writing. She is raising two children, Robert and Kennedy, with her husband Rob. Her writing interests are very diverse but definitely center around mystery and suspense. Active projects reflect her deep interest in genealogy.

Between the Lines

by Lyssa Menard

Erin's precocious publishing success masks
the meaning of her words.

1

yes squeezed tight, hand over gaping mouth, Alice failed to stifle a yawn. Erin waited in the interminable receiving line, watching as Alice endured several conversations with self-professed fans whose adoration must have been annoying. Erin could practically hear Alice thinking, "Where is my story?"

For the umpteenth time, Erin wondered whether her own story was worth telling. She discreetly checked her compact mirror. *At least I put myself together for this occasion.* Her waist-length mane of blonde, stick-straight hair had the cohesion and sheen only possible to generate with time and effort. A contoured dress showed off her slender frame and erect spine—the product of childhood ballet lessons. She was often told that she looked much younger than her forty-two years. *Not as young as the proverbial kid inside me, clamoring to be heard.*

Wrenching her attention away from her muddled inner dialogue, Erin noticed Alice fiddling with her charm bracelet. *I'll bet every charm has its own history—a story far more interesting than I can deliver.* Alice was fondling a particular charm. *It's a book. So apropos.* It was silver and looked solid and weighty, replete with meaning.

The line moved forward. It was finally Erin's turn to meet-and-greet but she hesitated to interrupt Alice's thoughts. Something about Alice's distant expression suggested that she was inside some meaningful memory. Erin waited a moment before slipping her hand gently into Alice's and entwining palms and thumbs.

Alice's attention rebounded and she grasped Erin's hand. She looked at Erin with a penetrating stare and curious expression, as Erin stood in front of the table.

I'm looming over this poor woman, Erin thought before sliding into the chair to speak with Alice at eye-level.

"I want to respect your wishes," said Erin, "so I'll refrain from boring you with my praise for your novels. But I do want to express my appreciation of the life you've lived aside from your writing. You're an excellent role model."

Alice's quizzical expression spoke volumes. "Who are you dear, and what do you know about my life?"

"How rude of me. My name is Erin Neuman and I'm a professor here at Northwestern."

"Oh, I've heard of you, Dr. Neuman," Alice exclaimed. "Aren't you the 'CEO Whisperer?'"

Erin laughed in surprise, a good, solid guffaw, and Alice chuckled in response.

"How in the world did that ridiculous moniker make it to your ears?" Erin asked, feeling a warm blush sprout on her cheeks and chest.

Alice smoothed her floral dress with a flourish and said, with a sassy smile, "You know that I read, dear, don't you? I don't just write. And I'm old, but I'm not dead yet!"

Erin nodded with another laugh. "Touché. Yes, one of my clients dubbed me the CEO Whisperer during a CNN interview and I've never been able to shake it. Once CNN labels you, you're stuck for life, but I do have to admit, as embarrassing as it is, it does have a nice ring." *Oh, lord, she probably thinks I'm a flaming narcissist now.*

But Alice's deep blue eyes seemed to brighten.

Erin bathed in the glow for a moment. *Maybe I won't disappoint her after all.*

"I have a question," Erin said, segueing away from discussion of her professional persona. "While you were on stage, I thought I saw you grimace for a moment. I noticed your expression just as a memory of my own first writing 'success' washed over me." Erin flicked her fingers in the universal air quotes gesture. "Did I imagine that, or were you having a bit of a flashback yourself?"

"Well, yes, CEO Whisperer, you did catch that wave, but I'm much more interested in hearing about your experience. Will you tell me your story?"

"Of course." She paused. "I have to warn you, though, this isn't a story with a happy ending." Erin looked at Alice with a solemn expression. "Are you sure this is something you want to hear?"

Alice nodded her head with more force than Erin would have expected from a centenarian. "Happy stories are boring, dear."

Just then Eddie brought them each a cold drink. "Gran's taken an interest, so you might be here for a while." He said it teasingly, and pecked his grandmother on the top of her head, looking for all the world like a parent with a particularly exasperating two-year-old.

Alice swatted him away playfully, affection flowing from her like a palpable current. "You're on," she said to Erin with a focused stare. She shifted in her seat. It seemed to Erin that Alice was making herself comfortable, settling in as if she was about to curl up with a good book.

"OK, then. Nothing like a bit of pressure." Erin took a deep breath. "Here goes…." She cleared her throat, slipped into her professorial tone, and began to deliver her story.

"Eleven-year-old Erin, constantly in trouble for her loquacious ways, was fitted for a high-tech muzzle by her father. Only he had access to the on/off switch, removing all semblance of control from the child and teaching her a powerful lesson about 'good' behavior. Children should be seen and not heard."

Alice looked appalled, but Erin quickly continued.

"That was the premise of my first published work—a supposedly fictional short story featured in a national magazine when I was twelve."

Alice sighed with relief, nodded, and gestured for Erin to continue.

"Everyone was thrilled with my precocious publishing success—teachers, principals, parents, friends. I was the talk of my hometown. But the sad truth is that the whole episode was actually a failure." Erin took a deep breath to steady herself. After a moment, she continued. "The meaning of the story

43

was lost in the excitement." She looked away from Alice, off into the distance, absorbed in a mental re-run of childhood events. "I don't know how conscious I was of this at the time—I can't remember, but I do know that this was a subtle plea for help. Apparently, too subtle."

Erin tensed and Alice leaned in closer, comforting Erin without invading her space.

"It still shakes me up to think about it but, in a figurative way, the story was true." Erin paused again, swallowing, holding back tears with great effort and little success.

Alice squeezed Erin's hand.

"I'd already been silenced by my father for many years at that point," Erin said. "He had drummed into me that family problems were meant to stay in the family. Problems like abuse and neglect were meant to stay secret. Of course, every perpetrator finds a way to demand silence, and my father was very convincing. Both he and my mother were abusive, though in different ways. The details aren't important. The critical point is that the abuse continued in silence until I was old enough to fight back and then, old enough to leave that house forever."

A few errant tears defied Erin as she struggled to choke them back. She wiped them away, both hands swiping her cheeks impatiently. "Everyone missed the point of the story." An audible twinge of resentment slipped out within the grief.

"I don't need any more details than you want to share, dear," said Alice. "As fresh as your pain feels, this story is tragically as old as time." She took both of Erin's hands in her own and squeezed, giving Erin time to collect herself.

"You asked for a seminal story and this is mine," said Erin. "I learned a lesson on a grand scale. Countless people read that story—people who knew me personally and people who didn't—but no one picked up the pain, the desperation, the hint that something was terribly wrong. The lesson I took from this was simple: I'm on my own; no one sees the pain and no one will intervene." She sighed. "I also came to the conclusion that there was no point in writing. I never published a personal work again. I lost my voice."

Alice's eyes were simultaneously focused and moist. She looked like she would leap from her wheelchair in fury if only her old body could. "That must have been so painful…and lonely."

"Well, on the positive side, the fact that no one took me seriously when I was in need led me eventually to my life's mission: to be there for others; not just to listen to their stories but to hear, to validate, to give love freely. And the more I give that presence, acceptance, and love to the leaders who work with me, the more those qualities trickle down. From me…to them… to their families and employees…and on down the chain. I've got miles to go in my own work, but it's healing to know that I've helped others."

Alice cocked her head. "I hear a 'but' coming."

"But, I look at your life—your success as a writer, of course, but also your success as a wife, a parent, and a grandparent. That's actually what I admire most about you. Watching the way Eddie treats you…well, let's just say that those loving interactions tell me all I need to know about the kind of person you are."

Erin's color drained and her eyes clouded over. "As for me…I've never been able to really let people in…to let others help me…to take a risk and give them a chance. Being abused by both a mother and a father does such a number on trust. Men can't be trusted. Women can't be trusted. It's a quandary." Erin shook her head. "I've missed out on love and family. I thought it would be easier as time went on. That I'd age out of sorrow about not having children. But now, I realize that I've missed out on grandkids as well. Like your Eddie." Erin sighed. "A whole new layer of pain and loss."

The two sat in silence, holding hands. Erin sensed the press of other well-wishers and the background chatter was audible. But the two seemed to be encased in a private bubble and neither was in a hurry to move the line along.

Erin broke the silence. "So, when I caught that moment of pain in your eyes, I immediately wanted to hear your story. And I suddenly felt a longing for advice from a woman both seasoned and wise: What do you do with your pain? How do you let people in?"

Alice kneaded her hands, massaging visible knots of arthritis, her eyes closed as if she was centering. Then, her attention returned. "No one escapes pain, dear, and I've certainly had my share. The truth is that life marches on for us all. You can't change the past. But you know what you can do? You can change the present. So let's start there, shall we?"

Erin felt confused. What was Alice saying?

"Tomorrow. Noon. My kitchen," Alice continued. "You'll bring your sad story and I'll bring mine. We'll have an intimate private reading."

It took a minute for Erin to metabolize the charming invitation but, once she did, she felt a wave of relief wash over her. "First we'll share. Then we'll heal?" she asked.

"Yes. And then, we'll write," Alice added. "I can't give you kids and I can't manufacture love—though Eddie's on the market and he's really quite a catch." She winked. "But, together we can use our stories to heal ourselves. And when our readers see themselves in our stories, we'll help them heal, as well." Then, softly, "It's time to reclaim your voice."

Erin's heart raced, first from fear, then from longing. Her eyes blurred and she squeezed Alice's hands. Alice squeezed back. In a swift cascade, every muscle in Erin's body released. *This is how safety feels.*

They embraced.

"Thank you for trusting me with your story, Erin. Now we're connected— a community of two. And we'll take it from there."

—— LYSSA MENARD ————————————————————

...is a clinical psychologist, business coach, and an assistant professor at Northwestern University. Writing has been her life-long passion, manifesting in published lyrics, short stories, and journal articles. Though she hasn't completed a book just yet, she's working on two and enjoying her fantasy of seeing them in press!

The Play

by Melissa Ann Weidner

A young addict sees her life in a stage play.

To: Erik, a wonderful person.
Never stop caring or daring
to dream.

"You can only lose something that
you have, but you cannot lose
something that you are."
—Eckhart Tolle

Love,
Melissa Ann Weidner

O

Ophelia was excited and a tad bit nervous as she approached Alice. She wiped the sweat from her palms. She was in her forties, pleasantly plump with light brown skin and long, curly dark brown hair. She was neither tall nor short and wore a pink and black coordinated outfit with zippered high-heeled black boots, and stood proud with a smile. There was a large colorful pin on her sweater that read, "Playwrights Know How To Play Right!" She held an extra pin in her hand and offered it to Alice when her turn came.

"Hi, Alice, my name is Ophelia Threadgoode. I've waited years to thank you for inspiring me to be the person I am today," she said as she approached Alice with extended hands. "I saw your play, *What Goes Up*, years ago and it changed my life."

Alice smiled as she accepted Ophelia's handshake and the pin, "I've heard of you! There's been some buzz about your work."

Ophelia beamed with pride and started on her story without delay, taking Alice back to that day when Alice unknowingly planted the seed for her life change.

ε ε ε

Ophelia was eighteen years old and asked her boyfriend George to accompany her to a play at a local independent theater in Logan Square. She read about the play in a theater newsletter and it struck a chord deep inside her.

They had been cooped up for two weeks doing little else besides drugs and each other. The world had become a hazy fog and the drugs were no longer fun. Somewhere in the haze, she realized George's "Trust me" mystery drug was crack cocaine and by the time she realized that, she was hooked.

"Fine," George said. "We can go see a stupid play, but only on the condition you take what I give you, smoke with me, and give me some satisfaction."

"Deal," Ophelia said. She naively accepted the oval blue pill he handed her and swallowed it down with some vodka ginger ale. Next, he lit up a joint, took several hits, and passed it to her. She enjoyed the strong herbal scent of the marijuana and puffed on the joint several times until her muscles felt relaxed. Her face flushed crimson from the alcohol. George pulled out a clear bag containing what looked like a couple of off-white rocks. He took the crack cocaine "rocks" out of the bag and mashed them into powder using the blade of his utility knife. He separated the powder into two lines. He snorted the bigger line and Ophelia snorted the rest.

"Good girl," George said as he roughly pressed his lips to hers. Then he whispered in her ear, "Now suck me, Baby."

Ophelia giggled. The crack made her feel giddy and hyper-aroused. She unzipped his pants and obliged.

When they arrived at the theater, Ophelia was still overly excited and her heart pounded rapidly from the cocaine. The sober part of her was impressed with the venue. This acting troupe had managed to settle down in a nice little storefront they turned into a theater. The auditorium had a small stage surrounded by forty folding chairs.

"What a shithole," George complained while they waited in the lobby.

"You don't find the place wonderfully intimate and creative?" Ophelia said. "I sure do! This theater is wonderful! I am so excited! I can't wait!"

"Damn, shut up crazy woman." George squeezed her arm much too hard. They entered the auditorium and took their seats.

When the play started the stage lit up and showed a mattress on the floor. The lights became brighter and revealed a woman lying on the mattress, blood dripping from her arms. Pill containers, drug paraphernalia, alcohol bottles, and knives were strewn about. A man sat near the woman and sobbed into his hands. A sad melody permeated the air.

Ophelia was entranced. Her eyes couldn't look away from the stage. Her mind flashed back to a few days earlier when she and George had a gun held to their heads and had been robbed by a fellow addict. Since they didn't get their fix that day, things had turned dark fast. George screamed at her and blamed everything on her. She screamed back at him. He slapped her hard in the face and locked her in the bedroom for several hours. Later that night Ophelia experienced horrendous stomach and back pain. She washed down a handful of pills with a bottle of vodka, cut herself on her arms, and cried herself to sleep. At that moment, she had wished it would be eternal sleep.

The play took the audience back in time, to when the two characters met, and followed their downward spiral. Their relationship was eerily comparable to Ophelia and George. The characters became co-dependent and mentally unstable, addicted to heroin, and lived in a haze. The woman in the play suffered tremendous physical and emotional pain, just like Ophelia. The relationship of the characters unraveled quickly.

The final scene went back to the opening scene. The man crossed the stage toward his lover lying on the mattress with all the bottles, drugs, and weapons strewn about.

"Dammit, Grace! Fuck! Not again," he shouted as he knelt down next to her. He took her listless body in his arms and sobbed, rocking back and forth, repeating the word *no* over and over again.

The lights went out, the play ended. Ophelia felt confused, with a rush of emotions tearing through her. She felt despair, joy, sadness, and hope all at once. Teary eyed and clapping, she glanced down at the playbill in her lap. The title was written in large, bold red lettering: *WHAT GOES UP*. Below that were the words *by Alice Bainbridge*.

Ophelia imprinted that name into her brain and turned to George, who appeared unmoved.

"I think I want to write a play now," said Ophelia as she wiped at her tears. "I *need* to write something like this. I want to write a play expressing the darkness and suffering I feel. And maybe I need to find something to hope for."

"Yeah, sure. Whatever you say, Babe," said George. He grabbed Ophelia by her arm and said, "Personally I found it a bit of a bore. Now wipe off those silly tears and let's get the hell out of here. I'm losing my buzz."

They got into the car and George immediately pulled out the cocaine and his utility knife. He snorted a line and offered Ophelia some. Ophelia looked down at the line in front of her and suddenly felt as though she didn't want the drugs, but she was scared to say no to George. He never accepted no as an answer from her. He held the line up to her face. Feeling torn, Ophelia snorted the line. George lit up a joint and they took turns puffing.

Feeling high and invincible, Ophelia gathered the strength to say what had been on her mind.

"I think maybe we should talk about going into rehab," said Ophelia. "Before we end up like the woman in the play."

His face contorted into a repulsive sneer, "Fuck you, bitch, I ain't going to no fucking rehab." He snorted another line and held more coke up to Ophelia's face. His arm shook and she couldn't tell if it was from the drugs, or just pure rage. Most likely it was a combination of both.

"Please, George," Ophelia pleaded as she placed her hand on his shaking arm, using all her might not to cave in. Her mind was screaming, *snort it!* But her heart was screaming, *get help!* "We have a serious problem."

"I don't have a fucking problem. You do." He leaned across her and swung her car door open, then pushed and kicked her to the curb and drove off.

Ophelia broke down in tears as she crawled to the sidewalk. Her mind was spinning. She looked at the cuts and bruises on her arms and craved another hit of the cocaine. *I must get home and beg his forgiveness. I must get home to satisfy him. He'll take me back. Wait, what the hell am I doing? He's a jerk loser. Must see him. Must go home. I must, I must, I must. George, why did you leave me here alone? Please Universe, show me a damn sign!*

As she sobbed, a vision of the dead woman from the play flashed in her mind, followed by another vision—this time, her own body lying dead on the sidewalk. A new resolve swept through her. *I will not die this way. I refuse to die this way.* She noticed the playbill lying beside her on the sidewalk. An ad on the back page read "James Treatment Center: We treat the whole person. Mind, body, and spirit." *This must be a sign*, she thought.

A taxi pulled up and the cabbie asked Ophelia if she was waiting for a ride. This was definitely a sign.

"Yes, yes I am," she said. She wiped away her tears and entered the taxi. "James Treatment Center please."

ε ε ε

"So you see," Ophelia said to Alice. "You not only inspired me to write, but to also live my life on my own terms. Clean, creative, and sober. I owe you everything."

Alice took Ophelia's hand in hers and pulled her into a warm embrace.

"Your life lessons will live on in the hearts of people like me for years to come," Ophelia said. "Thank you, Alice."

— MELISSA ANN WEIDNER —————

...is a medically disabled writer on a mission to help others. She published a poem at age 15 and has been writing ever since. She's currently working on a book about mental and physical health stigmas, and collaborating on a novel. She has volunteered at OCWW in many capacities since joining in 2015.

Hal's Story

by Thomas Sundell

Young Hal's father walks out on the family.

9

Hal and Sally decided to line up to greet the conference's ancient honoree. More Hal's idea than Sally's, though he couldn't have said why he wanted to greet Alice Bainbridge. As the line moved slowly forward, it became apparent that the old woman gave some people short if polite shrift while others got more attention.

Sally said, "This is taking too much time."

"You could go on," said Hal. "I'll stay in line. I know you are more interested in meeting publishers and literary agents."

Gesturing at the fellow lingering with the honoree, Sally said, "Seems like Ms. Bainbridge really does want to hear stories."

"Yeah, what would you say to someone a hundred years old that could possibly interest her?" he chuckled. "She's lived through so much. Born in 1919, which means she experienced the Great Depression as a teenager and World War II as a young adult. Her first book published in '39, as war broke out in Europe."

Sally agreed. "The Cold War, Kennedy assassinated, Civil Rights, the Viet Nam War—wasn't she a famous protester during that war? I think I read that somewhere."

Hal nodded agreement, given Ms. Bainbridge's plays—more polemical than the novels. The novels mostly centered on the foibles of family life, of tragedies within the domestic circle.

Sally said, "You stay if you want. I'm going to the vendor hall. I don't know what I'd say to her anyway."

Twenty minutes later, Harald's turn finally came. "Ms. Bainbridge, pleased to me you. I'm Harald Malmquist. Call me Hal. You asked for stories so I'll give you a bit of mine." He waited for her reaction.

A dry handshake. He took care with the small, parchment-thin hand.

"Please do, Hal." Her watery blue eyes on his. "Weren't you in line with a younger woman?"

"Yes, my colleague, Sally Dent. We split responsibilities. She's gone to meet the publishers."

"So I'm your responsibility," said the old lady wryly, a hint of a smile in her eyes.

He chuckled, unsure why he felt nervous. "Well, I'm just half your age, but I want to tell you of something from when I was twelve, going on thirteen. It was during seventh grade, the second school I attended that school year, because we recently moved from our house in the suburbs to a rented duplex in the city. If I recall right, we moved in February and this was the end of March.

"I came home from school for lunch and found my dad hurrying down the walkway with two suitcases in hand. Heavy, from the looks of them. All he said to me as he went by was, 'Look to your mom, Hal,' which made no sense since she was at work.

"My brother Bernie was in high school, a junior. So there was no one home, the house empty; I guess I'd be called a latch-key kid today. Anyway, I ate my lunch and went back to school. After school I played outside with some friends, it being a warm day for early spring.

"When I came home at supper time, Bernie said 'Where have you been? It's six o'clock.' I could see he was worried but I wasn't sure why. Mom was due home at any time.

"Turned out Dad left an envelope addressed to Mom, really to Phyllis, her name. Only it was unsealed and Bernie had read it. He said, 'Dad's left Mom. Left us.' And sure enough, my brother showed me that Dad's clothes were gone from their closet and bureau. Other things of Dad's gone. Everything, like shaving stuff. Tools from the workbench. His guns. Some of the mystery novels he'd read. Just everything. No wonder Bernie was freaked.

"I told Bernie about seeing Dad at lunchtime. Thinking then maybe Dad was going on a business trip, which he did from time to time.

"Bernie said, 'You know Mom isn't herself lately,' which was also true. I guess she did okay at work, but at home she mostly read the Bible, forgot to get supper, sometimes didn't talk to us at all. Sort of in her own world. Started a year and a half before, when the baby was stillborn. Would have been our sister.

"Mom arrived home, sort of operating on automatic. Bernie showed her the letter from Dad. Didn't seem to mean anything to her. She just went and got her Bible. Bernie and I ate bologna and cheese sandwiches for supper; we each made our own. Applesauce for dessert.

"It went downhill from there. Mom didn't get up for work the next day. Wouldn't get out of bed the rest of the week, except to use the john. Wouldn't talk to us. Only slept or read her Bible. She must have eaten, I guess, but if she did it was in the middle of the night.

"I asked Bernie, 'What were we going to do?' I'd gone to school on Thursday and Friday, but come Sunday night, I wasn't sure I wanted to go on Monday. Bernie said, 'We've got to call Grampa or Aunt Frannie.' I voted for Grampa. Aunt Frannie was kind of a stickler for decorum; that's what she called it.

"Bernie made the call, explained what'd happened. Grampa told him, 'Sit tight. I'll be there by Tuesday afternoon.' We were living in Nashville, Tennessee. Grampa was in western Pennsylvania and Aunt Frannie in Washington, D.C., where she worked for the government."

Looking at the others waiting to talk with Ms. Bainbridge, Hal said, "Well, I'm holding up your line." He added, "Let me just say, Dad leaving ended our family life as it had been. My mother went into an institution for two years. Bernie stayed in Nashville to complete high school, and then went into the army. I lived with my Grampa over his shoe store. He fixed up the attic to be my bedroom. I didn't see my dad again for twenty years."

Ms. Bainbridge raised a finger, "Over thirty years ago, right? What I wonder is how did you deal with it? What impact has it for you now?"

Hal hesitated, then said, "I shut down, too. Sort of like my mom, shutting down my emotions. I guess so I wouldn't be hurt anymore. Turned into a reader. Read every book in Grampa's home and a lot of the books at the local library. I think that's what started me on the road to writing."

She asked, "Did you re-learn to feel emotions?"

A tough question for Hal, "Yes, pretty much, though it took years and two failed marriages."

She nodded, "I understand. Thank you for sharing with me, I do appreciate it. Let's see how you do over your next fifty years. Still time for a successful marriage." She pointed with her chin, "Your friend Sally is back, looking for you."

Hal thanked Ms. Bainbridge for listening, unsure really why he'd felt compelled to tell her of that time when he rarely considered it anymore. As he walked to Sally, he thought about the troubles his colleague had gone through. Late thirties, divorced, a youngster at home. He liked her but had been wary of anything more personal than business and casual exchanges.

He wondered if asking Sally out could be construed as harassment. Well, they were peers at work, at least. He figured he could ask. If she said no, then that would be that.

THOMAS SUNDELL

...is the author of *A Bloodline of Kings* (Crow Woods Publishing), translated and published in Greece as *Philip of Macedon* (Minoas SA), and sixteen other novels. Formerly an HR consultant, now retired, he writes each morning and sketches most afternoons. His novels and short stories can be found at sundellwritings.wordpress.com.

The Pacifist

by Susan Levi

A young girl's self-concept is challenged by a
fight with her best friend.

10

"Hi Alice. I'm Deborah and I have a story and a question for you." Deborah smiled with self-satisfaction. She doubted many others ahead of her had followed Alice's instructions to skip the thank you and adorations.

"I'd love to hear them," Alice said.

Deborah wasn't convinced. The older woman looked like she was ready to doze off. How could she have thought this famous author could be interested in an untold story from fifty years ago? It was hard to tell with those drooping eyelids, but it appeared Alice's eyes were still open, so she set her copy of *Revelation, Remorse and Restitution* on the table and launched into her story:

ε ε ε

Even in the sandbox little Deborah never fought back. Greg stole a shovel right out of her hands and she picked up a different toy, as if she didn't care. Deborah didn't. Her father coached her to fight for the shovel or defend her castle from attack. There's even a home movie where dear old Dad threw sand in her face when she gave up a toy to him. Parenting was different in the Fifties, but her mom must've known that was over the line because she turned off the camera. Her mom bragged to friends and family that Deborah was a born pacifist, a peacemaker, and very fond of appeasement. Her dad didn't want her to be a pushover, but he relaxed as Deborah learned to proactively share and engage her playmates in creating castles and construction sites together.

On Owl Drive, boys dominated the neighborhood. By first grade, Deborah was recruited to play army, cops and robbers, or cowboys and Indians, but Deborah refused a gun or any weapon and became the compassionate nurse, always at the ready to cross enemy lines to help anyone injured or to broker a truce. She puffed up like a proud chameleon when her parents or neighbors told these stories. Deborah had found an identity that pleased and suited her, despite the low status and eye rolling from the other kids that came along with it. She cared more about adult approval anyway.

During second grade, her family moved to Arlington Heights and Deborah stayed with the next-door-neighbors after school until her parents came home from work, just after the Garfield Goose Show. Caroline, who was in the same class as Deborah, and her little sister, Julia, loved to sit at the kitchen table and play *Mensch argere Dich nict*, the German version of *Sorry*. Deborah and Caroline both reveled in the game's playful ruthlessness and quickly became best friends. Deborah never knocked out little Julia, so she could still feel like a pacifist and do-gooder. Caroline's mother smiled in her saintly way and served them Tang, just like the astronauts drank. "Thank you, Mrs. Schultz," Deborah said while Caroline mocked her for her politeness.

When the girls played house, Deborah played orphanage, lining up Thumbelina, Chatty Cathy, Little Miss Echo and assorted other orphans in cardboard beds lovingly lined with the softest towels and linens. She always let Julia adopt Thumbelina. In third grade, when her friends played school, Deborah set up a residential school, complete with charts and strategies to redeem even the most incorrigible students. She was a pacifist and proud do-gooder, after all.

In fourth grade when the girls played *Sound of Music*, Deborah insisted on being Mother Superior while the other girls took turns being Maria. This demoralized her Protestant mother. Deborah's pacifist, do-gooder, holier than thou identity didn't win many friends, but her best friend Caroline stood by her.

Caroline and her little sister Julia loved putting on shows as much as Deborah loved choreographing them. They danced with high kicks in a three-person chorus line, roller skated elaborate routines, and sat with knees turned and ankles crossed on the wood post fence between their yards, serenading the flowers. When they tired of the variety show format, Deborah wrote plays that typecast the girls so they loved their roles. She always gave Caroline, who loved being the star, the biggest part.

That all changed in fifth grade, when Caroline attacked Deborah in her own backyard. Deborah had written a poem about Caroline's mother's garden, which was published in the school anthology.

"You can't write about my mom!" Caroline screamed. "She's my mother, not yours!"

"You're just jealous they picked my poem and not yours." Deborah said with a righteous Mother Superior tone.

It was a logical assumption. The two girls were competitive with each other and it generally brought out the best in both of them. But Caroline let her know she had it wrong that time when she yanked Deborah's hair, forcing her to her knees.

"Owww! Let go," Deborah said.

"Say you're sorry!"

Deborah had nothing to apologize for. She tried to pry Caroline's fingers away, but Caroline just pulled harder.

"You're gonna pull my hair out," Deborah said.

"Apologize!"

Not an option. One of Caroline's long braids dangled in front of Deborah's face. Her fingers prickled and her ears burned. Deborah pulled that braid down so hard Caroline dropped to the ground, screaming and swatting at Deborah. The girls tumbled over and both let go.

"I had to do that," Deborah said. "You were hurting me."

They scrambled up to their feet and circled like pro wrestlers, but there was nothing fake about what was going on between them. Caroline charged and Deborah retreated with quick backward steps—but not fast enough. Caroline grabbed Deborah's perfectly pressed button-down blouse and ripped it open. Buttons flew everywhere and her just-budding breasts were exposed. Deborah felt a cold wave of shame followed by a hot rage in her cheeks. Forsaking her pacifist principles, she yanked Caroline's blouse open, rejoicing in the sound of popping buttons and the sight of them sailing into the air and disappearing into the green grass. This sent Caroline running and crying to her mother. Deborah was a latchkey kid and sniveled her way into an empty house, awkwardly pulling her shirt closed, alone.

ε ε ε

"Alice, I really was a good person until that moment," Deborah said, steeling her gaze on the book at the center of the table, determined to avoid the judgment she feared in the wise woman's eyes.

"And what are you now, my dear?"

"Someone pretending to be a good person." Deborah said. "At that moment, my life changed. Everything I knew about myself was no longer true." She looked into Alice's kind eyes. "How do your characters find their redemption?"

"Did Caroline ever forgive you?"

"Yes, years later," Deborah said. "I finally understood it wasn't about the poem."

"What was it then?"

"She thought I was poaching her mother." Even now it was hard for Deborah to admit this was true, though she hadn't done it knowingly at the time.

Alice nodded. "My characters forgive themselves, but I'm not surprised you didn't notice that."

"Why not?"

Alice signed Deborah's copy of *Revelation, Remorse and Restitution* and slid it toward her. "You could read this again or write your own book." Alice's blue eyes brightened. "Sometimes it's best to learn from your own reveal."

SUSAN LEVI

...is a retired educator channeling her creative energy into writing fiction. She is revising her first novel, *Damascus Rose*. Susan has taken writing classes at StoryStudio in Chicago, including Novel in a Year with Abby Geni. She serves as Co-Director of Programming and Manuscript Coordinator for OCWW.

Gabriel Bryant Bruce

by Michael Farley

A litter of words left behind.

11

Bryant sat still, breathing slowly, thinking about Alice, who had invited him to tell a story only he could tell. His story. He sat at her table and bent over from the weight of this opportunity, his face almost touching the table top.

Bryant brought himself upright and gathered his personal items, then hesitated. The room roiled with raucous excitement, with voices colliding off walls and ceiling. The tumult pressed down on his shoulders and leadened his unsteady steps.

"Maybe I should skip this and head out to the conference room for the breakout sessions and workshops," he thought to himself.

Walking toward a group milling about Alice, basking in her radiant glow, Bryant stopped.

Looking into the conference area he saw the exit sign and others walking by on their way to sessions. He took a deep breath and then stepped in line to speak with Alice.

Time slowed and all movement fell away into a gentle pause.

Her voice was soft and welcoming. "Hello, what is your name?" Alice asked.

"My name is Gabriel Bryant Bruce, but I go by Bryant," he said. May I sit down?"

"Of course you may, Bryant. Tell me your story." She reached out to touch his hand and he saw that the skin on her hand was like melted wax, with a white translucent glow.

"I want nothing more or less than to be able to do what you are asking Ms. Bainbridge," he began.

"Alice…call me Alice."

"Certainly, Alice. But before I begin my story…"

Alice's eyes began to look away. Bryant smiled and brought her gaze back to his eyes, and he said to her with love and admiration, "I feel like my life has been a long path to this moment, a moment to thank you for your generosity of heart and the immensity of your inspiration. Never did I ever imagine I would be able to sit here across from you and share this story. And Bryant began.

ε ε ε

"My life has been one long battle with words.

"Written words have been my enemy from the time I first became aware that words could be read and spoken. To me they were indecipherable, symbols without meaning or any sense at all. I would ask my parents, cousins, older brother, or anyone who could read to read to me…so I could enjoy the stories, comic books, funny papers, and I kept asking far past what was considered time for me to begin reading.

"At first this didn't bother me. In fact I simply thought that at some point, like magic, I would know how to read.

"My mother was a first-grade teacher and so it wasn't long before she saw that there was a problem. I was not achieving at the level an "average" child would, so by the time I was in second grade I was called out of the classroom to be tested.

"When I was called out of the room, I was confused and embarrassed. There were many questions, and different puzzles to solve. I didn't know a lot of the answers and often it took me a long time to come up with the right ones. The psychologist was friendly and smiled a lot, reminding me that I should take my time. When the session ended she told me she wanted to see me again for the next few days.

"It was a humiliation to be the only child to be called out of the room to take tests that no one else had to take. I felt small and wanted to disappear completely from view. I felt all the eyes of my classmates watching as I walked up the aisle and out the door.

"After the testing was done and life in school returned to normal, I forgot about the times I was taken out. I was content with my reading group, although as a Blue Bird I knew that I was in the lowest reading group in the class. Red Birds on top, Robins second and the Blue Birds at the bottom. And I was at the bottom of the bottom.

"Many weeks later my mother sat down with me and said she had news about the tests that I had taken. She said that they were to test my intelligence, they were called IQ tests, and that I was average in most of the areas, above average in one, and below average in ones that involved reading.

"Because of that, I needed to go to a remedial reading teacher to get help. She seemed happy and said that all she ever wanted was good average children. I guessed that I was a good average child, except for reading.

"What they didn't know at the time the tests were given and interpreted is that I had a learning disability. The approach in remedial reading was to teach phonics, which was like trying to help a blind person see by putting glasses on them. My brain was not capable of deciphering the code of sounds written words were divided into. But I tried, and tried, and flailed about…failing more than succeeding.

"School was like having all these books piled on a sledge to pull across a rocky path while all the other kids had their books on a wagon with wheels to pull easily over the terrain, and then there were some who had a Red Radio Flyer Wagon, leaving everyone in the dust.

"I learned to not raise my hand, not expect to get recognition, not to try because I would be apt to fail and disappoint, and be disappointed.

"I struggled through high school and went to college in Wisconsin, where I continued to struggle. While I was there I took a class in Shakespeare's plays where I learned to appreciate storytelling and the secret language of metaphor, symbolism and rhythmic uses of language.

"I was only able to begin to read this complex and difficult early English writing after discovering recordings of actual Shakespearean plays in the

University Library. I listened to them, as they were acted out, and I would follow along with the printed word.

"What I walked away from college with was not a degree, but an appreciation for Shakespeare and a desire to write poetry.

"Over the past 50 years, I have written thousands of poems. No one has seen any of them. All placed in a chest. All attempts to use words to describe the feeling and things of the world in ways which were meant to bring those words alive, and glow as the fullness of life itself…"

ε ε ε

Bryant blinked, as if coming back to the here and now. "I'm sorry Alice," he said, "I think I've rambled on a bit, and I believe my time is up…"

Alice had been attentive and she reached out to take Bryant's hands which were now balled into a tight knot on the table top.

"You have the soul of a poet…and the fear of a child, lost." Alice spoke with eyes holding Bryant's. "You are like an athlete who has trained in solitude. Working tirelessly to become competitive but never competing. Never seeking a coach to guide you, to give you criticism and challenging you to succeed. Never running in races to measure yourself against others, as well as yourself. If you are serious you must take those steps, as all serious people do.

"It doesn't matter what you write, or if you achieve fame or fortune, but without submitting your writing to be published you will die with a life incomplete."

Bryant saw Eddie walking over to move him along and he began to stand up.

Alice, still holding Bryant's hands, spoke, "Bryant, send me a poem. Eddie has my contact information." She took a deep breath, "My husband was a poet, and I would love to read your writing. Thank you for your inspiring story."

Bryant stood and turned to leave, then suddenly stopped and turned around to the questioning faces of Alice and Eddie.

"Alice, may I take one more minute of your time? I have a confession to make."

Bryant didn't wait for an answer but sat while Alice leaned back in her chair and Eddie started to come around to Bryant's side of the table.

"It's okay Eddie. Go ahead Bryant, please continue," Alice said, still looking quizzical and laying her hands on the top of the table.

"I know your husband was a poet, I have read his poetry as long as I have been reading your books. In fact, his poetry influenced me greatly."

"Last night, I was thinking about today."

Alice nodded slightly and smiled as Bryant paused.

"I couldn't help but think about your husband, Jonathan, and the love for you he shared in many of his poems."

Both Alice and Bryant were transfixed, eyes welling.

"As I thought about this love I began to write a poem, a humble gift, inspired by your husband…and by my desire to give you both my gratitude."

Bryant reached into his notebook and took out an envelope and handed it to Eddie, who had moved back to Alice's side.

"Thank you for taking this time with me. I will leave you now, and believe you will feel Jonathan's influence when you read this poem later."

Bryant gathered his things, trying to contain his emotions. Walking up the aisle he heard Alice say to Eddie in a voice already choking. "Read it to me now, Eddie."

Bryant stopped as he heard Eddie begin:

> Listen to this
>
> These words long to speak
> Complete only with you
> in this evening's
> reach of gentle tree's
> branches
> brushing this day
> into twilight

Hear that slight sound
Aloft
Wrapped so soft
around
this cool
sweeping of sky

Around this faint cry
of shadow's
dusk

This slip of fleeting quiet's calm

A psalm
of breath
rests

here

I await

Unwashed and unworthy

~Gabriel Bryant Bruce

Bryant turned to see Eddie kneeling down to hold Alice in his arms as she silently sobbed into his shoulder, unable to contain the flood of emotions Bryant's poem brought her. The sight of Alice caused a hot stream of tears to pour down his cheeks, dripping down his chin and onto his coat.

Wiping his face with his coat sleeve Bryant walked out of University Hall and was greeted with the clear cold air of winter along the shore of Lake Michigan. The setting sun revealing a landscape of frozen mist and sleet that encrusted the campus and trees and homes and streets, light now reflecting off the sheen of ice covering this world with amazement and beauty.

Bryant had to hold on to the iron railing as he went down the steps toward the remnants of rose-colored clouds strung along the horizon. He moved slowly, carefully, but decidedly, step by step negotiating the glazed cement and then the slippery stone path.

Going home.

— MICHAEL FARLEY

...is a retired public relations and advertising executive, and longtime foodie. His love of language and creative writing lead him to a lifetime of writing poetry and that has now expanded to include short stories and novels. OCWW has been a springboard for him to submit his poems for contests and publication.

Alpha Dog

by Teri Lavelle

A rambunctious dog humiliates
thirteen-year-old Megan.

12

"Well, hello! Nice to meet you and all that!" Alice greeted Megan. "Let's get down to business." She leaned forward in her chair, gripping its arms, and looked Megan in the eye. "I'm Alice, and I'm a writer. What's your name?"

"Hello, Alice, my name's Megan, and I'm thrilled to meet you. I'm a huge fan, of your writing," Megan said. Her eyes were watering, then she sniffled and dabbed her nose with the back of her wrist.

"What's wrong? Do you have a cold?" Alice asked.

"No, I don't have a cold, Alice. It's just that you look like my grandmother. I'm sorry for the tears. She and I were close, but she passed away two years ago in June," Megan said. She reached into her purse and pulled out a tissue.

"Sorry about your grandmother, Megan," Alice said. She paused for a few seconds, while the young woman wiped her nose. "So, young lady, what's your story?"

"My story happened to me in junior high school."

"That's the worst time in a child's life, don't you think? Horrible time. So, let's hear about you and your junior high school story."

"My junior high school was located in the foothills of the coastal mountains on the San Francisco Peninsula. The school was a splendid example of mid-century of architecture, as the school's main structure slashed horizontally into a steep hillside, and the building had no interior hallways."

"No interior hallways? That is strange," Alice said. "What if it rained?"

"The roof extended out over the outdoor balconies, corridors, and walkways, so we did not get rained on. I don't think it'd be possible to have this type of school building in the Midwest. The design is called 'open-air concept,' and was famous throughout California in the 1950s.

"On the main building's second floor was an extended outdoor corridor. It ran parallel to about seven classrooms and was paved with a concrete walkway, and its length was bordered by a short retaining wall—which in fair weather served as seating for students waiting for class to start. Above this little wall was a thirty-foot grassy slope, and at its edge was a wire fence demarcating the school grounds from the woods and shallow lake beyond it.

"It was mid-January, and I had just turned thirteen. My most treasured birthday gift was a matching hat and scarf set from my beautiful and hip Aunt Penny. Married to my Uncle Paul, Aunt Penny came to our family gatherings dressed in the newest fashion and spent time with my sisters and me while the rest of the adults socialized and drank cocktails in the kitchen. She was my fashion idol and confidante. To this day I am still not sure if I loved that knitwear because it was stylish, or because my beloved Aunt Penny had given it to me.

"The knit set was made of tangerine mohair, and it was fuzzy, soft, and warm. The hat was small enough to fit snugly on my head, and the orange color brought out the auburn highlights in my long hair. The scarf was about six inches wide, and five feet long with orange fringe on either end. I usually wore the scarf in loose loops around my neck—mostly for its style in the mild San Francisco winters. I felt pretty in this ensemble, and this was a rare thing for me—a seventh-grade girl who stood close to six feet tall. Although I was tall, I was skinny, and my height made me awkward and self-conscious. I fantasized daily about being a different girl with unexceptional physical characteristics, so I could just blend in with the rest of my seventh-grade class."

"You were in California for junior high? That is interesting. You were tall, skinny, and angsty. Okay, but isn't everyone at that age? I'm tall, and I was tall in junior high, too."

"Just listen, Alice. It gets crazy. One day right after our morning recess, I took off my scarf and held it in my left hand as I walked down the long, outdoor corridor. When I reached the door to my class, I felt a fierce yank of my hand, and my fingers let go of my scarf. Then I saw a large golden retriever shoot past me with my scarf clenched in his mouth. That dog—who was long-eared and had large paws—sped down the corridor and up onto the grassy embankment above the corridor dragging my scarf on the ground. He then turned around, hurtling across the grass, and came back in my direction.

"He leapt playfully in the wet grass and shook the scarf so hard his ears flapped upside-down across his head. I jumped up onto the embankment and ran after the dog, calling for him to stop. When he did stop, he turned toward me and dropped the muffler on the grass between his front paws. Then he leaned back with his haunches high as though he were ready to pounce, but instead, he just wagged his tail and barked at me. When I lurched forward to grab my scarf, the dog snatched it off the ground and sprang further up the hill. He zigzagged, running at full speed with the scarf snapping behind him. I can't remember how many times the dog toyed with me by dropping the muffler and then running off again with it."

"You chased the dog? Why didn't you just wait until he tired to get it from him?" Alice said.

"I loved that scarf, and I was thirteen years old—you know, a little kid in a big kid's body," Megan said to Alice. "The chase was attracting quite a crowd. The dog seemed to run faster when the kids clapped and cheered. He widened his route by bounding further down the embankment from where I was standing and came back toward me. One time he made a pass a few feet in front of me, and I reached out to grab my scarf, but the dog and scarf moved past me too quickly.

"As it approached time for classes to start, the outdoor corridor was filled with about half the junior high. I knew that every single kid was watching me chase that dog for my scarf. I was tired from the running and embarrassed at having all the kids laughing at me. I almost started to cry. It was then I decided to give up the chase and let the dog keep my scarf. I jumped off the embankment and walked slowly back toward my classroom. I stopped and saw the dog from the corner of my eye.

"Soon after I quit chasing him, he stopped running and stood to look at me with the scarf in his mouth. After a few seconds, the dog dropped the scarf on the ground waiting to see if I would continue to chase him.

"I didn't do anything. I just stood in place and looked at the dog. The animal just waited in the grass, panting, for a few seconds. After that, he turned around, raised his right rear leg, and urinated on my scarf."

"No. That did not happen!" Alice said.

"It did happen," Megan said. "I think it even surprised the kids at school. When the dog peed on my scarf, the kids whooped and screamed for a long time, but the dog was calm once he finished his business. Afterward, he ran toward the fence and squeezed under it and continued into the woods. He was gone. A boy in my English class climbed onto the slope, grabbed my scarf, and handed it to me. It was filthy now with mud, dried clumps of grass, and dog pee. The bell rang for class, and all the kids dispersed to their different rooms. I walked into mine and threw the scarf into the wastebasket."

"That's a shame about a perfectly good scarf. Why didn't you just take it home and have your mother launder it for you?" Alice said. She had been leaning toward Megan and was so close that the younger woman could feel the air coming from her breath as she spoke.

"My friends asked me the same thing at the time. I could never wear that scarf to school again. It would have been recognized as the scarf that was peed on, and I would be the girl whose scarf was peed on," Megan said. "Quite frankly, wearing it again would have been social suicide for me in junior high."

"In my day, we would have worn the scarf again," said Alice. "We did not have money to waste on our pride, but I am sorry about your scarf. That was crazy. 'Life is stranger than fiction!'"

— TERI LAVELLE

...a native San Franciscan, is a published poet, and for three years, the author of a weekly marathon blog for a large running organization. Currently, she is teaching college freshman writing skills, submitting short stories for publication, and finishing her first novel. Teri is also the former OCWW Programing Co-Chair 2012-2015.

Wishing Well

by Paco Aramburu

A man's destiny is changed by an odd passenger.

13

As Enrico approached the table, his mind tried to connect the memories he had of her book *Highly Paid Insultants,* to this blue eyed, frail woman extending a long, slender hand to be taken.

"Why are you wearing sunglasses?" she croaked.

"I guess that is a consequence of one moment in my life that I would like to share with you." He looked around to make sure there were no intrusive ears to pick up what he was about to tell her.

"Is it a confession?" She smiled sadly.

"Of sorts. I'm sure you know this: in everyone's life there is a moment that changes everything. The one that changed mine didn't look like much to everyone else at the party in 1995."

ع ع ع

"It was at a swanky penthouse with a view of Lake Michigan and through the floor-to-ceiling windows you could see the night lights outlining Chicago's darkened beaches. There was a woman I was interested in. At first, I thought she was fascinated with my conversation, but after I came back with drinks, I saw her slender fingers resting impudently on the wrong arm, the hairy arm of a guy that she had obviously chosen for his bulk. I actually heard him blurt out: 'amanarchitect,' when she asked him a question.

"I admit to some sour-graping. I rationalized about young women choosing to endure some abuse and lies for the ancestral need to be physically protected. That's when the shift occurred. Entirely in my mind and unnoticed by everyone else. My perception rendered what had been a fun gathering of loosely acquainted people into a frivolous excuse to drink and behave as much like animals as alcohol allowed. A moment ago, I had been one of them, and I would have been delighted to engage in the ritual alienation of myself; but I had observed them in a different light. This new awareness prevented me from participating. I left with a dejected sense of superiority and alienation.

"From the sidewalk, I raised the collar of my raincoat to fend off the cold wind and welcomed the lone walk on Oakdale Street. Looking for my car, I noticed an old Toyota Corolla parked on the street that looked exactly like my first car. I smiled with affection. With a brownish green body and beige interior, it made me remember the brand-new thrill of driving my own vehicle. My amusement turned to surprise when I saw, parked behind the Toyota, a blue Gremlin identical to the one I had bought from an Armenian fellow. That had been my second car, a small step up. And behind them, the beige Oldsmobile that had succeeded the two, and the old Buick Park Avenue!

"I tried to make sense of this impossible alignment of all the cars I owned in my life, in order. Was it possible that the world made sense? Could this order reflect a secret structure, an implausible wizardry aimed at confusing me alone on a dark street?

"When I saw my actual car—a silver Chrysler—for a second, I felt better, until I realized someone was sitting inside, a man. As I approached, I could make out a ruddy, fat face framed by salt-and-pepper hair cropped short. He lowered the window and smiled benignly.

"I asked what he was doing in my car.

"'Waiting. For you,' he said. He searched inside his leather jacket and handed me a business card that read: *Concession Sanctioning of America, Aloisius Strowling, Predilection Management Consultant.* No address, no phone number.

"I insisted. 'What are you doing in my car?'

"He simply looked at his hands as they lay in his lap and waited. I re-read his card, but the words didn't make any more sense the second time.

"Before I could react, he blurted out, 'She was going to get pregnant, that girl was. You're thinking with the right head, Jack.' He gave me a crooked look. 'Come on in, you wanna talk to me.'

"I crossed to the driver side, turned on the ignition and inspected my smiling passenger.

"He said, 'She was going to leave something else for you.'

"'What do you mean?' I waited for a response, but all I got was the stranger arching his eyebrows. 'The kind you cure with penicillin?' I asked.

"'You wish.'

"'HIV?'

"He nodded. I blame my slow reaction on the beers I had at the party. The two or three neurons still working managed to shoot a couple of questions. 'Who are you? And how come you know me, but you call me Jack?'

"'Read my card?' His fat finger pointed to the white rectangle still in my hand.

"'Yes. It doesn't make any sense.'

"'Don't get so hot, Jack!'

"'My name is not Jack, it's Enrico.'

"'You know how things go. No card, no name, no job ever makes sense. Right? In my line of work…ain't no room for guesses. I'm in the wish granting business.'

"I chortled, waiting for a punch line. But he stared at me with blue eyes as calm as a wading pool. 'Are you with the Grant a Wish Foundation? Because you come into my car—'

"He interrupted with 'Too straight, Jack. I'll just grant you three wishes. No papers, no records.'

"I choked back my laughter. 'Wait…wait, hold on a minute. Do you expect me to believe this nonsense? What are you, a genie?'

"'I like Predilection Management Consultant.'

"'And the consultant part comes where?' I asked him, hoping to understand.

"'I help people choose carefully.' He pointed a finger at me; then continued: 'You're laughing. Hear me out, okay? Most guys don't really get the power in wishes. A good wish, a really good wish, is like a piece of future boxed in your head, ready to be opened.' I smiled, and he nodded. 'Dat's right.'

"'You mentioned clients. How much is this going to cost me?'

"'See? We're consulting now.' He pointed a finger and a smile at me. 'This thing, it'll cost you everything you have.'

"'You mean my student loans, my rent, my car payments, my medical bills—'

"He stopped me with his hand, took a couple of seconds and began, 'it's gonna cost you everything, and sure, your debts too.'

"'So why would I want three wishes then?'

"'Hey, Jack, you play the way you want to; I only make it so you can play.' He looked at me with those eyes, and for an instant I doubted myself. In that moment I wondered if the road had come to the fork. My passenger turned, faced somewhere in the distance and sighed.

"'But what about my cars? Look! Right there, those are all the cars I ever owned, in the order in which I purchased them! Did you do that? Why?'

"He sighed again. As if talking to a particularly slow student, he said, 'As I hit my knee,' his hand slapped his leg, 'two kids are born, a man dies, thirty-two thousand married men are being cheated on, sixteen virgins lose their cherry for the second time and ninety-seven million people snore. Because you go to a fancy party, thirty-three people die in six cities. Could've been avoided if you'd stayed home. Right now, all the change you own adds up to exactly five dollars. Just now, when you discovered your old jalopy, you lived exactly one billion seconds. You get it Jack?'

"'Enrico. Get what?'

"'Let me tell you. Some guys can hit a little ball with a stick, and they do it so good that they make a lot of dough. Others are good at figuring odds.'

"'And you are…?'

"'Wadda you think? I'd be sitting with you here, talking to a clueless guy in a car? No. I can figure the odds on anything. On anybody.'

"'So, with me you figured…what?'

"'You gotta go straight home tonight. Don't talk to nobody. The way I figure is that I grant you and you're in. Three wishes. That's it Jack.'

"'So how do you do it? You work with God, angels, the Devil, Bill Gates? Is this like *It's a Wonderful Life?*'

"'No! Listen, nobody knows how come you were born here and not in Calcutta, right? You cross the street a million times, but another guy gets squeezed by a bus—'

"'Yes, but how can you know?'

"'Why the Hell do you care? I dunno why this or that happens. I dunno how come you were a billion seconds old when you saw that Toyota or the change, or the girl with HIV—'

"'But, but…all the cars I owned, in order—'

"'Hear me this: when it comes to why, what's the meaning of life, we humans are like an old record: all we can do is go round and round playing our song, but we don't know who's listening, we don't know who bought the record or if they like it, and for sure we don't know who owns the record player. We just play. See? Dat's what I'm saying. You don't get it, but you have three wishes comin' to ya. Nobody cares why! You got your three. What you gonna do?'

"'And if I give you my three wishes, you'll leave my car?'

"'Ha! I'll be gone before you finish your third.'

"'Okay so it's time to get started.'

"'No time like the present.'

"'I'll start with…oh I don't know, sixty, wait! Eighty million dollars.'

"'In the trunk, baby!'

"I excused myself and opened my trunk. The wind blew a hundred-dollar bill into my hand. The trunk was filled with money, practically to the top. Another bill blew away. I closed the lid and my eyes. I replenished the air in my lungs and walked slowly to my seat. After fixing my raincoat, I watched my passenger for a while.

"He muffled a yawn; then said: 'Two to go.'

"'Okay, okay. I'll go with health then.'

"His hands made an arching gesture. 'Jack, you can't go wrong with health.'

"I took a deep breath and pronounced, 'I want to be healthy forever.'

"He beat both knees with his hands. 'Good! One more and I'm gone. You never see me again.'

"I thought about being irresistible to women, but I imagined all the complications that would entail, so I asked to be quite attractive to women. He unceremoniously let himself out of my car, and without a word, walked clumsily down the dark street until I lost sight of him.

"I noticed my fast breathing as my attention returned to the car. I had just lost and acquired an unknown number of expectations. My old aspirations had just become obsolete and I had yet to create new ones, more appropriate to my new position. The future, my future, had just become a lot less defined, but it was now full of promises and questions about my adequacy with the newly acquired wealth. When I let go of my breath, I realized how tired I was. All I wanted was to sleep and to let events unfold."

Ș Ș Ș

Alice had a small smile and a twinkle in her eye. "Are you happier now, behind your sunglasses?"

"Without restrictions, I embarked on a campaign to take care of every need I ever had. I thought of myself as an errant collection of desires waiting to be satisfied. All those trinkets I couldn't afford before, all sorts of amusements forbidden by my previous lack of money were bought and soon discarded. Those women who I couldn't date in the past gravitated to me like moons incapable of breaking from my orbit.

"My soul melted as if looking for a container, a form to inhabit, a frontier to guide its new shapelessness. At one point I couldn't recognize myself. Taking inventory of my acquisitions I found myself definitively in the red."

Spent, Enrico sat back and let a breath escape.

Alice patted his hand and said, "Remember this, sometimes the light hides the candle." She sat back and nodded as if going to sleep.

Not knowing what to do, he thanked her in a whisper and walked away, incapable of paying attention to anyone else. As he searched for his car in the parking lot, he wondered what she meant by the light hiding the candle.

— PACO ARAMBURU

...is an adoptive son of Chicago, a writer, and a recovering graphic artist. He has published short stories, has written two novels, and is working on a third: *Falling Into Perfection*, a dystopian Chicago story in an alternate reality. Paco is OCWW's Vice President and Director of Marketing.

Millie

by Fred Fitzsimmons

A great short story writer's dying wish.

14

Jessica Hawkins checked into the Orrington Hotel in Evanston exhausted from her day of teaching and a harrowing, delayed flight from Iowa City to O'Hare. Though fatigued, sleep escaped her. She couldn't shake ruminations over the mission ahead in her morning meeting with Alice Bainbridge. Reflections arose without relief regarding her departed friend, Mildred Rawlins. Thoughts about their connection bore a mix of fondness and disappointment. A deep pang of guilt continued gnawing at Jesse over her delay in delivering her promise to her colleague. She tossed and turned in bed, each recollection of her unfulfilled commitment to Millie burdening her with desperation.

ε ε ε

Jesse took the measure of the five steps up to the dais and rehearsed her message as she approached Alice.

She slid into the chair across the table from her host. "Hello, Ms. Bainbridge. I'm Jessica Hawkings. Everyone calls me Jesse. I'm delighted for this chance to meet you in person. I can't tell you how impressed I am with your novels. *The Quicksand of Life* and *The Sparrow Flitted and Flew, the Eagle Soared* are my favorites. I reference them often in my classroom and workshop instruction."

"I'm pleased you found them helpful, Jesse."

"I also read your latest, *Revelation, Remorse, and Restitution*. The story is terrific, so deserving of the National Book of the Year Award."

Alice thanked her, then asked, "Jesse, your name is familiar to me. Did we cross paths somewhere?"

"You and I share a connection, a mutual friend, Millie Rawlins."

"Oh, of course," said Alice. "My gracious, yes, forgive me. Now it all comes back to me. You're the young lady from Iowa City about whom Millie told me so much. She said you and she developed a close friendship, and you devoted a great deal of time to help her bring her novel to finish. The poor girl, only seventy-five, she died at such a young age; I miss her. We remained dear friends for fifty years. What a shame she departed without seeing her book published."

"Yes," sighed Jesse. "It shattered her."

"How terrible."

"I believe the defeats she experienced hastened Millie's end," said Jesse. "She and I connected seven years before and became staunch friends. An association by happenstance; a friendship struck when she attended my lectures, at the University of Iowa's annual Summer Writers' Workshop. She liked my presentations and returned yearly until her death."

"What a fortunate coincidence."

"I agree," said Jesse. "Millie stood forty years my senior, but we possessed much in common. Love of story-writing, consumption of the rich works of literary geniuses like Joyce, Hemingway, Fitzgerald, Faulkner, Poe, Bronte, and others. Each of us also embraced the satisfaction of tutoring novices on creative writing. Work with budding writers gave us, Millie, in particular, an uplifting sense of accomplishment providing insights for beginners into the craft they loved."

Alice raised her hand in a friendly manner and wagged her large-knuckled, arthritic finger at her visitor. "Now, Jesse, no more of this formality, please call me Alice. We too are now friends. Like you, I remember how much time Millie devoted to the education of young writers. She prided herself in sharing her knowledge of the profession with those who strived to improve their writing."

Jesse nodded, smiling. "And Millie was also a brilliant short-story writer and essayist. Her writings appeared in the most prestigious literary journals in the U.S. and around the world. The recognition she realized for her stories, the respect, acclaim, and awards she gleaned for those achievements gave her a sensation of gratification and self-worth beyond compare. Still, as you know, her great regret for twenty-five years was her inability to write a successful novel. That frustration left her unfulfilled. She confessed to me that her frustration in not succeeding in the long-fiction format crushed her. She held a yearning to be an acclaimed novelist, like you, her best friend. Her disappointment, in this regard, bred her emptiness and distress."

"I never comprehended the gravity of Millie's wound," said Alice. "By what you tell me, her setbacks with her novel caused her misery."

"Her suffering pained me," said Jesse. "Unhappiness dragged her down to depths I had never encountered in her. She knew I coached, critiqued, and edited the work of prominent authors, so she asked my help, along with yours, in her novel-writing. I consented and toiled with her, as did you, on draft after draft of changes, rewrites, and corrections over the five years before her death. Collaboration is what brought us so close together. Toward the end, her finished text met the approval of both of us for publisher submission. The final touch included your suggestion for an important change in the final chapter. Her prose, in my estimation, scored worthy of a Book of the Year Award, and I told her so. Labored achievement in overcoming her writing albatross, at last, rewarded her with the delight she fought so hard to achieve.

"But failing health in her final days stifled her joy. She came to understand her written work wouldn't see publication before her passing. She clasped my hand during our last conversation and implored me to shepherd her manuscript through to publication. That was two years ago, but I still haven't been able to carry out my commitment to my friend."

Alice nodded solemnly. "You've both endured a lot."

"Alice, I never should've promised Millie what I lacked the time and talent to deliver. I'm ashamed to say, teaching duties, speaking engagements, and publishing requirements left me insufficient time to pursue her book's publication to the extent necessary, to fulfill my promise. My facility in securing placement for so many of my short stories with literary journals also gave me an unwarranted hubris. And my agent made placing my novels look easy. It led me to believe I could do the same for Millie's novel. I showed myself wrong, ever so wrong. I've proven to be a miserable failure at representing her work. The few publishers' doors I opened a crack slammed shut quickly—what an embarrassing learning experience!"

"You tried hard on her behalf, Jesse, but you faced overwhelming hurdles."

"That's what drew me to consult with you, Alice," said Jesse. "Millie trusted and relied on you as her beta-reader, coach, critic, and editor. I hoped I might persuade you to help satisfy her last wish. Your influence with your book publisher, and with your agent who has such great status in the industry, could get her work in front of the right people. Would you help connect me with sources willing to consider Millie's story? What a wonderful gift this would be to your best friend."

Alice perked-up, her spirit renewed.

"I knew two years ago Millie's health was fast failing," said Alice, "but I didn't realize her death was imminent until her family called to tell me she had died. I hadn't received any word from her about my suggestion for the last chapter change. I thought she decided not to incorporate it or had given up hope of finishing the book before she passed. This is the first I've learned of her incorporating my suggested edits for the final chapter, and that Millie wished to have her book published posthumously. I had no idea that was her wish."

"Your suggested final chapter edit was the clincher in Millie's mind," said Jesse. "It convinced her that the book was complete and ready to submit for publication."

"I'm humbled," Alice said. "How kind of you to think of me in this way. I saw Millie's book blossom over the years with each revision. I'm sure you had much to do with it, Jesse. My last reservation with her novel had been the final chapter. Based on what you've told me I can now put that reservation aside. Of course, I'll help you if I can. Perhaps together we can double our chance of succeeding."

"I can't tell you how much I appreciate your willingness to assist!" said Jesse.

Alice beamed. "Jesse, a thought strikes me. Both my agent and my editor are here at the event. Did you bring a copy of Millie's novel with you?"

"Yes, and some pitch materials."

"Eddie! Eddie dear! Would you ask my editor and agent to join us?" Alice called to her grandson. "Tell her we possess something important for her to consider, the last work of a celebrated author. Tell them I believe one of their competitors will snap up the book if they aren't quick to take on its publication!"

Jesse rested her hand with tenderness on Alice's. "Alice, you now understand why you are here."

   ℰ ℰ ℰ

Drained, Jesse flopped into her seat upon boarding her plane home. Notions swarmed from her discussion with Alice. She basked in the vision of Alice's joy as she listened, enthralled, to hear her editor react to their pitch for Millie's novel.

"The book's subject matter has strong reader appeal," the editor had said. "The characters sound compelling, and the tonal approach is refreshing. I also like the title, *Adversity to Conquest*. I'm only going on your pitch and the plot synopsis and what I know about Millie's other work, but I can't wait to dig into the full manuscript."

Jesse thought, *Millie ached for recognition for her novel. She deserved the attention she will now receive for her work.*

And Jesse marveled at the irony that the title of Millie's novel so perfectly reflected the real events in her life: she had written through adversity, and now her work was poised for publishing acceptance. A triumph for her, thanks to her friend Alice.

—— FRED FITZSIMMONS ————

...is President of OCWW. He has several flash fiction/short stories in circulation for publication. He is also exploring agents for his debut novel *The Green Office,* a character drama about an ambitious young executive whose life spins out of control when he joins a corrupt firm.

Memories Awakened

by Cathy Chester

A homeless woman cuts to the truth in
Cindi's life.

15

Alice's tired voice queried, "Well, you coming?"

Startled, the middle aged, troubled writer looked up and saw that the room was nearly empty. Wearing the compulsory jeans and t-shirt, trying to fit in, she questioned why she was even there.

"Sorry, didn't mean to keep you." The woman drifted toward Alice.

"C'mon girl, I don't have another hundred years to wait," urged Alice.

Questioning if her uncertainty was wasting Alice's time, the woman slowed her steps even more and muttered, 'Not worthy, not worthy.' Her thoughts went to the line from *Wayne's World*. Sad how once degraded, you always seem to remain that way, particularly to yourself.

Seeing the less than enthusiastic facial expression, Alice probed, "Why did you come today?"

"Honestly for some credit. Our lit prof said we should come. Something about filling seats and a whole bunch of reasons that didn't make sense."

Alice chuckled, "Well, that's the most candid answer I've gotten in a while. So, what's your story?"

"Well, it's a story about the people Cindi sees on the CTA elevated. Intertwined is a story about a young girl on a train obviously being bullied. The main characters are…"

Exasperated Alice interrupted, "I didn't ask for the backstory I just want to hear the *story*."

An almost inaudible voice whispered, "Sorry, maybe I should go."

Alice's head shot up and threw a stare that made the woman start talking.

ε ε ε

Mary and Cindi met waiting for the CTA Red line, known to locals as the 'L'.
Mary greeted her with, "You a Cubs fan? You sure dress up like one."

Cindi remembers laughing as she responded, "Yeah, a lifelong fan, but this
is my uniform."

Wide eyed and a bit louder than Cindi anticipated, Mary gushed, "You work
there? At Wrigley? What a gig! I once met Ernie Banks. Billy Williams, too!"
Her enthusiasm reminded Cindi why she loves working at Wrigley Field.

As the L approached, Mary started gathering multiple bags. "Do you need
help?" Cindi normally wouldn't have asked, but she felt drawn to Mary for
some reason. "Where are you headed?"

"Wherever the L takes me," said Mary. "Heat in the winter and air condi-
tioning in the summer, you can't beat it. You learn the stations where the better
bathrooms are, and the Dunkin' Donut shops that give you a cup of coffee or
some left over donuts. This line takes you from Howard Street to 95th Street,
which is almost the entire length of Chicago so I can sit for a good stretch of the
day. One day though I'm moving somewhere where it's warm. This old body
just can't take the winters anymore."

Awkwardly Cindi realized that the 'L' was home for Mary. A line from an
old TV program came to mind, 'There are eight million stories in the naked city,
and this has been one of them.' Little did Cindi know what she would learn by
people-watching on the L.

A few days later, Cindi saw Mary again, and Mary couldn't contain her
excitement. "Cubs won the other night, saw the flag flying. Whoever thought of
that idea sure was smart. Instant messaging long before this so-called Instagram
stuff. They should have patented the idea. They'd be millionaires!" Mary belly-
laughed at her own joke. Even on her worst day, Mary found something to
laugh about. Unassumingly, she made the best of her situation.

The L was ready to pull out of the Granville station, and Cindi heard a
scream echoing in the stairway. "Hold the train." Just as the doors are about

to shut, a ruffled woman jumped on. Her bag was sticking halfway out, but with a firm tug, it followed her momentum. Most people didn't even notice, Mary did.

"Never knew I'd be such a trend setter."

Mary saw the quizzical look on Cindi's face. "Look at her pants. Just like mine except my tears and shreds come from daily use, not a designer's scissors." Mary shook her head and brushed at the holes in her jeans. "Do you see how she hugs that designer bag? Must have some pretty valuable stuff in it. The only time I scrunch my bags like that is late at night when I think I might fall asleep. I've got some valuables in my bags too—everything I own."

Mary picked up her plastic Target bags. She wasn't making a joke. For the first time, a look of sadness came over Mary's face. Releasing the grip on her own backpack Cindi realized just how strong a hold she had. For what? From whom? Another lesson from Mary; it's not the valuables but the value.

The Cubs had a long road trip, so ten days elapsed before Cindi saw Mary again. They smiled and sat together on the train.

Cindi noticed a young girl sitting alone, staring out the window, seeing nothing but reflections of another day. Standing nearby was a group of kids. One of the boys stuttered mockingly, "Hey, Sssssally. How wawawas sssssschool tototday?"

She ignored him and slipped further down into the seat, the reaction of a girl who has learned the hard way that it's better to ignore than to react.

He continued, "Dididid your MMMom mmmake that outfit or dididid you bbuy it at a thththrift store?" The group howled. A bitchy girl, dressed in the shredded jeans of Mary's angst, got into Sally's face, "Next time you might want to wash it before you wear it or is that stench coming from you?"

Cindi noticed Sally curve her hands into balled fists. She felt she should go over and help but knew that would only make things worse. Cindi recognized that sad expression, complete with its hidden emotions, covered arms, and lost thoughts. She had been in that reflective image and would never forget what it is like.

Cindi slumped in her seat, clenching her fingers into long-forgotten fists. "That is so wrong!"

Mary shrugged her shoulders and said, "So, go do something. People see things but don't do anything. Do what you know is right. It's not about you."

Cindi internally fought the reflection of her past and knew Mary was right. She positioned herself between Sally and the group, hoping that a blocking adult would save Sally from more taunts.

Cindi also saw Sally scratching some old scabs, making them bleed. She remembered that feeling of release as the blood slithers down, and she unconsciously touched her own upper thigh. *Cutting calms you, allows you to breathe. The initial rip of your skin, the blood oozing, releasing your inner evil.* The scabs and jagged scars allowed her to survive each cruelty.

Through pursed lips, Cindi hissed, "Stop it, you bunch of self-absorbed, self-centered, over-privileged brats! Can't you see what you are doing to her?" They just turned around and laughed. Cindi heard the phrase pulsing in her head, "We were just kidding."

Cindi wanted to pass her cell number to Sally and tell her to call, yet she felt that she'd just be seen as a crazy lady who should learn to mind her own business.

As she got off the L at Addison, Cindi nodded toward Mary. Before going down the stairs, she paused and thought of Mary, the lives of people on the L, and her own doubts. Colors raced through her mind and, like pulling into stations, the blurred colors became words. Change one letter and suddenly scare and scars become one.

Cindi looked for Sally the rest of the baseball season, but the kids were on summer break. She hoped Sally was okay, away from those bullies, at least until school started again. She didn't see Mary the rest of the season either. Mary looked tired and didn't have the same essence last time Cindi saw her. Cindi hoped Mary had moved to that warmer climate. The image of Mary would always be a reminder of how much more Cindi should do, even as she fought her own fears.

ε ε ε

The woman ended her story and waited for Alice to say something.

"So which one were you?"

With amazement and confusion, the woman looked away from Alice and mumbled, "Both. I was that girl bullied in school wishing that I could just end it all and I started cutting. And I'm Cindi, wishing I could stop worrying about what others think of me all the time." Her voice grew stronger as she added, "But most importantly, I wish I could be Mary with the strength to accept who I am."

"Don't we all," Alice said haltingly, "don't we all? Thank you for sharing your story. Gives me a lot to think about."

CATHY CHESTER

...is a retired teacher having an array of experiences for forty-two years. She renewed her love of writing through the Society of Children's Book Writers & Illustrators and joined OCWW in 2017. She is also involved in a children's poetry critique group. OCWW has led her to a budding interest in flash fiction.

The Week That Was

by Della Leavitt

A teen-ager's first trip to New York
during a world-changing week.

16

My hands shook as I awaited my turn to speak to author Alice Bainbridge. I had admired her since high school when my best friend's mother introduced me to Bainbridge's books, along with those of Doris Lessing and the music of Billie Holiday: all artists I treasure to this day.

And now, *the* Alice Bainbridge wanted a story from me?

When I reached the front of the line, I sucked in my gut and let the words tumble out.

"I'm Dina Jacobson," I said. "Ms. Bainbridge, you're among my favorite authors ever. In the last five years, in addition to reading, I've embraced a writing life. Although I feel privileged to do so when my peers are planning retirement, it's hard to be a novice again."

Alice's eyes bored into mine. "No matter what our experience," she said, "we all begin anew every day." She paused, then, asked, "Now, what story do you have for me?"

I took a deep breath. "It's about a single week, over fifty years ago, that transformed the world and changed me."

Alice surprised me with a smile. "You've made me curious, my dear; please go on."

"Thank you," I said. "Knowing you want to hear my story means a lot to me."

I closed my eyes and went back to those days.

ε ε ε

During my last year of high school, I practically lived in my best friend Maya's home. I wasn't estranged from my loving parents, but as the oldest of their five children, I yearned to escape our crowded house. Maya and her family beckoned, offering me worldly tableaus to explore those confusing times that included the civil rights movement, the draft, escalation of the war in Vietnam, and of course, sex, drugs and rock & roll. So much was changing at a time when I was unsure about who I was and who I would become.

Maya's family discussed politics and social issues. In my home, the topics never strayed beyond extended family concerns and our welcoming suburban synagogue community. My parents' subscriptions to three Chicago newspapers, *Reader's' Digest, Time* and *Life* magazines failed to satisfy my curiosity about the tumultuous world.

Civic leaders and people who had gone underground during the McCarthy Communist witch hunts were all dinner guests in Maya's home. They debated Mary McCarthy's book, *Vietnam*, and the risk of hosting meetings for GI's who opposed the war. Their discussions excited me, but I felt shy to participate, although the adults urged me to speak up. Soon I became emboldened to express my opinions, and my voice emerged away from my family's tame Shabbat dinners where we chanted blessings before meals of steaming chicken soup and tangy brisket.

When Maya's mother invited me to accompany her and Maya on a spring break trip to New York City, I really felt like a member of the family. My dad paid my way and I kept track of my share of expenses. Maya's mom, a stout, graying matron, was the best tour guide I could imagine. She knew her way everywhere.

At Rockefeller Center we took the elevator to the free observation deck with its stunning views of the Empire State Building and Lower Manhattan, and then lined up at theatre box offices as soon as they opened to buy tickets to carefully-selected Off Broadway shows. We visited Cooper Union, the Met, Whitney, the whimsically-designed Guggenheim museum, Brooklyn Botanic Gardens, and rested in the public library. Maya and I were high school cheerleaders, but her mom kept us running, and we often begged her to let us take a cab.

Her mother ignored our pleas. "Keep walking, girls!"

All my life, I hear her words urging me on.

The three of us shared a small hotel room with twin beds and a rollaway. On Sunday night, March 31, 1968, we crowded around the TV to watch a special address from the Oval Office. The last lines from President Johnson shocked us, "I shall not seek and I will not accept the nomination." We cheered. No more LBJ!

The next day we were shut out of our tour of the United Nations because the building was closed to tourists. As we stood on the sidewalk pondering where to go next, the presidential limo rounded the corner. We were amazed when LBJ himself waved to us from behind lightly-tinted windows on his way to what would be a failed effort to broker his promised peace treaty with North Vietnam. As he drove by, we shouted and pointed to the white, turquoise, and navy blue *Gene McCarthy for President* buttons plastered on our coats, proving our support for the anti-war candidate, although were still a few years shy of voting age. We showed him! End the war now! Maya and I felt we knew everything.

On Thursday morning at the diner across the street from our hotel, Maya and I schemed to order hamburgers for breakfast. With a laugh, Maya's mom surprised us by giving us the okay before our subway trip to the tip of Manhattan and paying the nickel fare on the Staten Island Ferry. Afterward we stopped for a snack at an automat, and took the bus uptown toward the Cloisters. As we rode, I stared at the man seated opposite me holding a tabloid-style newspaper in front of his face. The full-page headline assaulted me:

MARTIN

KING

SLAIN

Martin King? Who was he? A New York mobster? It couldn't be *The Reverend Doctor Martin Luther King*. No one ever referred to him simply as, "Martin King." People around us had been silent, but soon all jabbered with the news. The unthinkable tragedy was true, and we quickly got off the bus. For the first and only time, we took a cab back to our hotel.

That night, Maya, her mother, and I huddled around the hotel room's TV screen again, this time watching in horror images of riots all across the country. On the west side of Chicago, where the three of us had volunteered the previous summer in a preschool Head Start program, fires burned and people ran through the streets. I cried and wondered where our three year-olds were that night. It was clear I lived more than a world away from them, separated by a chasm I could never cross.

I felt powerless and angry. If our generation didn't change this unjust world, who would?

On Friday we went to the Museum of Modern Art where one room was devoted to Picasso's immense masterpiece, *Guernica*, over twenty-five feet long and eleven feet high. I sank onto the bench in front of the painting, feeling insignificant facing this passionate expression of the horrors of war. Our teen-aged anti-war fervor felt like a futile game. Captivated, I sat transfixed, searching each section of the piece, sitting for I don't know how long. I heard the horse neighing in anguish, while the stoic Spanish bull looked on. Women wailed. I saw blood. The outstretched arm held only a faint lantern of hope.

Maya's mom touched my shoulder and I looked up, relieved. I was safe with the only adult who could understand my distress.

"We'll be back," she said, as she left with Maya to tour another part of the museum.

On our last night, Maya and I awoke to hear her mother vomiting. We got scared, and Maya knocked on the bathroom door.

"Don't worry, girls," her mom called out. "I'm fine."

Was she? Had she been overcome, like I had been, by the shocking events of the week? I felt woozy. In the morning, we dawdled over breakfast at LaGuardia Airport. I was suffering, and said, "I think I'm having an identity crisis!" The new label for an old concept.

That remarkable woman, a decade younger than I am now, surprised me. "I'm still having one," she said, and gave me a hug. "It never ends."

Never ends? Not possible. Maya's mom was wise about social issues, art, music, and could fearlessly explore any neighborhood in every city.

By the time we reached the gate, our plane had gone. We couldn't go back home the same way we left. American Airlines rerouted us to Midway Airport, but Maya's dad was waiting at O'Hare. He had to drive fifty extra miles across the city and arrived furious. We had no excuses and didn't dare speak for the next hour.

When he dropped me at my home, my head spun. It all looked familiar, but strangely off kilter. My mother welcomed me as ever, now wearing a new blue housecoat to replace the yellow-flowered duster she had worn every weekday all year.

The world had changed in just one week and so had I.

The villainous president who we blamed for a never-ending war in Vietnam would be out of office in a few months. A great civil rights leader had been shot down and his loss cut deep, leaving a societal gash that had unleashed an eruption of Black rage.

And where did I fit? Yes, this was the beginning of my lifelong identity crisis, just as Maya's mom predicted.

ଌ ଌ ଌ

Alice looked up at me. "I remember that week, too, my dear," she said. "Of course, in 1968, I was closer to your friend's mother's age than to yours. I do know when you look back fifty years, memory works a magic of its own. True, those upheavals in the United States took place in a week that was like no other. You were lucky to have your friend's mother to guide you."

I brushed away a tear, missing Maya's wonderful mother who had succumbed to Alzheimer's disease twenty-five years earlier.

"I agree," I said. "Past events may become blurred, but the people we shared them with are unforgettable. They remain an indelible part of who we are."

— DELLA LEAVITT

...feels lucky to be writing when her peers are planning retirement. She had a lengthy tech career, taught mathematics, and earned her PhD in 2010 from UIC's College of Education. Her first novel, *The Measure of a Teacher*, is being reviewed by agents.

Welcome Home

by Lisa Sukenic

Dora's life begins with an escape from Nazi Europe.

17

Ruth Katz stood in line waiting to get her book signed by Alice Bainbridge. She didn't need to be first to talk to her, but she certainly did not want to be the last. After all, how many stories could a woman who was one hundred years old realistically listen to? She mindlessly fidgeted with the hidden compartment in her purse, making sure the paper and photo were still there. She hadn't asked her mom if she could take them. Mom wouldn't have noticed. Lately Mom repeated herself and did not remember what she had just said. Ruth debated about bringing her to meet Alice, but she was too unpredictable.

"Thank you very much, for sharing your story," Alice said to the woman before her.

Alice's voice sounded perfunctory and tired already. Ruth hoped that she had not waited too long and would be worthy of her full attention. Her grandson handed Alice a glass of water and a few tissues. Ruth held out her hand and Alice nodded and took it in hers.

"Ruth Katz, nice to meet you, Ms. Bainbridge."

"You can call me Alice," she said in a matter of fact tone.

"I've been reading *Revelation, Remorse and Restitution* to my mother and I'd like to tell you her story."

"How old is your mother?" Alice asked.

"My mother will be turning ninety, next month. Her story began in Munich, as Hitler was rising to power. He was kicking out all of the people without German citizenship. My grandfather had a Russian passport and my family thought it was awful being made to leave the country. This was the very thing that saved her life. My mother was scared, being only ten years old. She and her family took the train to Italy. She remembered seeing people throwing money out the window between the border of Germany and Italy. Years later she found out that they were worried they would be sent back if they had too much money. The steamship left from Italy and a month later the boat docked in Shanghai. They lived in a barracks-type room in Hongkew District that they shared with several families. The conditions were filthy and there was not much privacy.

My mother grew up in China and met my dad there, but it wasn't home. My dad was sent to a concentration camp and released. Eventually he wound up in Shanghai. My parents left when the war ended in 1947. They didn't want to go back to Munich. They had lost too much to return. When they were granted visas they went to live near her only surviving relative, Aunt May, who lived in Skokie, Illinois. My mom and dad were part of the eight thousand Holocaust survivors who were relocated here."

Alice inhaled deeply then spoke up "Your parents endured a lot."

"Yes, many of the refugees wanted to build a synagogue nearby but no one would sell the land to them. Eventually they had a third-party signer who was not Jewish. My dad no longer believed in God but he had to have the Jewish community around him since most of his family had perished. My parents tried to protect me, but the anti-Jewish sentiment came full force to Skokie in the Seventies," Ruth said.

Ruth took out a photo and handed it to Alice. Alice slowly lifted the picture close to her face, nearer to her glasses. She examined the photo of Ruth and her mom with a sign.

"This picture was taken at the protest in Skokie in April 1977, against the Neo-Nazis marching," Ruth said.

"What does the sign say? The print is so small."

"It says, 'Never again,'" said Ruth.

Ruth handed Alice the poem she found at her mother's house.

"I remember this," said Alice. "I read my poem *Welcome to America*. You know I was there at the protest…So much hate." Alice shifted in her wheelchair a bit.

Alice stared into the distance and began reciting the poem…

> *"We do not welcome everyone,*
> *not a melting pot,*
> *stones thrown instead,*
> *we look the other way,*
> *pretend to open our doors*
> *when…"*

Alice's voice started to strain and crack a bit. "I'm sorry, I can't remember the rest."

Alice handed the photo and poem back to Ruth, and she carefully placed them in her purse.

"I would have loved to have met your mother," Alice said.

"Mom needs to be at home with someone," said Ruth. "She's with Rachel today."

"Who's Rachel?"

"My partner of thirty-eight years. Lately it seems like Rachel is her 'favorite' daughter. It's easier for the two of them. Rachel seemed to be the truth serum for our family. She was Jewish and she felt familiar to them. My parents would tell her stories I had never heard. One time, my mother brought out their wedding scroll to show us. It had intricate Chinese characters inked on delicate rice paper with white plum blossoms painted in the background."

Ruth looked back at the long line behind her and realized that her moment with Alice Bainbridge was up. She reached into her conference bag and pulled out *Revelation, Remorse and Restitution* for Alice to sign.

"Who should I dedicate this to?" asked Alice.

"My mother, Ms. Dora Katz, please."

Her grandson stepped forward to help Alice. She was writing more than just her name. She closed the book and handed it back to Ruth.

"Thank you for sharing your family's story with me," Alice said.

Ruth walked away and found a bench to sit on and opened the book to read Alice's inscription.

> To Dora, you've had a remarkable life...Keep telling your stories. You remind us all to never forget.
> Fondly, Alice Bainbridge.

—— LISA SUKENIC ——————————————

...is a fourth grade teacher and a poet. She has completed a middle grade historical novel in verse and a picture book which are currently out on submission. Her poetry and haikus have appeared in *Everyday Haiku, an anthology* (Wander Muse Press), *Poems that Ate our Ears*, and *Not for Ourselves Alone*.

Sylvie Green

by Deborah Kahn

Sylvie deals with self-esteem issues.

18

ylvie stood in the chaotic horde of writers, unsure whether to stand in the long line, or come back when most of the crowd had left. She was here to meet Alice Bainbridge. Now, wrestling with whether or not to tough it out, she pondered what story to tell that would let Alice know how much she meant to her.

Her first novel just published, 23-year-old Sylvie had been so excited to meet her "mentor." She had imagined gently taking the bird-like hand of the frail centenarian and staring intently into her light-colored blue eyes. Alice would say to her, "Tell me your story, dear." And, with tears in her eyes, Sylvie would explain how Alice and her writings had changed Sylvie's life. Then she shook her head. How trite. As if every other writer in the room didn't have the same story, or some version of it. She was a writer, dammit. Couldn't she just create some interesting, off-the-cuff fictional piece to regale the elderly author? Sadly, that seemed to be beyond her at the moment.

Discouragement was starting to creep in. First, she'd had to sit through that boring presentation. Even Alice had looked impatient to have it over. Now Alice was besieged by hordes of mostly gray-haired writers, all wanting to meet her, fawn over her, and maybe tell her a story. She already looked tired. By the time Sylvie got to the head of the line, Alice might have expired from fatigue. Bleah.

Thirsty, she decided to get something to drink and watch the line from a distance. Her excitement warred with anxiety. She was such a new, untried author, her book just going on sale that week. She pinched herself every time she saw a copy of it. While checking to reassure herself that the signed copy of her novel and that precious book that Alice had written were still there, she clumsily dumped her bag. She dropped to her knees and frantically tried to retrieve her wayward belongings. Sylvie was startled when she felt a tap on her arm. Her apprehension turned to shock when she realized it was Alice's grandson, Eddie.

"Need some help?" He bent over, capturing a runaway pen.

Eddie was tall and balding and looked only vaguely like Alice. He seemed a comfortable sort in his plaid sport coat and open-collared shirt, smelling vaguely of vanilla. She had heard that men liked the smell of vanilla. Personally she found the scent slightly cloying and old-fashioned, but fortunately the aroma was faint.

"No, that's ok. I've got it." She held up the last renegade pen triumphantly, scrambling to her feet and pushing her straight black hair behind her ear, fiddling with the clip.

Eddie peered down at her, then over at the line of writers, then said, "Excuse me. I couldn't help noticing you hovering here. Are you just curious or are you hoping to tell Alice a story? You're so much younger than most of this crowd, I thought perhaps you're a new reader, hoping to have a book signed."

Wiping her suddenly teary eyes, Sylvie said, "No, I'm not a new reader. I do have a story to tell, but I'm not sure it's worth Alice's time."

"Is the story important to you?"

"Yes," Sylvie nodded vehemently. "It's the story of how I became a writer." Then, suddenly less sure, she added, "But I'm sure everyone here has that story. Alice will be tired of that tale long before I have the opportunity to speak to her." She could hear herself sounding flat and whiny at the same time. Bile rose in her throat as she thought of how cowardly she was. Come on, she told herself. You're better than this.

Eddie smiled and took her hand. In a kind voice he said, "Even so, I think my grandmother would like to hear it. And every writer deserves to be heard. What's your name?"

"Sylvie Green."

"And what do you write, Sylvie?"

Straightening and willing herself to sound confident, she told Eddie, "I just published my first book. It is a historical mystery about a murder in the Arctic during the nineteenth-century Franklin expedition, all fictitious of course. Mostly though, it's about how an unexpected experience can reshape lives, create new passions, and instill longing for a place that supersedes reason and common sense. It's about uncontrollable desire and the willing-ness to do anything and give up everything to appease that appetite." Her eyes were shining and her hands moved expressively as she recited her carefully crafted book blurb.

She saw Eddie's nod and looked again at the queue, still shuffling slowly.

"Fascinating. I'm sure Alice will want to hear your story. She's interested in polar exploration, and young writers," he told her.

Taking Sylvie's elbow, he urged her toward the table. "Alice," he said, "I think you'll want to hear the story that this newly published author, Sylvie Green, has to tell."

Sylvie looked down the long line of writers, all waiting for a turn. Alice would wear out before she ever got to the end. Alice sighed and motioned her over to the table. She took Sylvie's hand in her frail, arthritic claw and her penetrating gaze made Sylvie squirm.

Sylvie wet her lips. After a pause she blurted, "My mom got sick when I was in high school." Alice gave a minute nod of encouragement.

"She didn't die or anything," Sylvie hastened to add. "Anyway, uh, my life changed."

"Of course it did," Alice agreed.

"Oh, God, this is so boring. I don't know why I thought you would be interested."

Alice held out her hand for Sylvie to hold. "Just relax, dear. Let your story unfold however you like."

Nodding, Sylvie continued hesitantly. "Everything changed that year. I didn't have to take care of Mom, but my sisters were younger and I was expected to watch them, and I did some of the cooking and other house-work." Sylvie fiddled with one of her pens, clicking the point up and down. "Anyway, with all that going on at home, I didn't have time for much else. No time for friends, clubs, movies, dates. My life was a desert." She fell silent.

After a while, Alice prompted, "Go on dear. The natives are restless."

Sylvie shook herself out of her torpor. She could see a hint of impatience in Alice's eyes. "Sorry. Ah, well. Things went on like that for a long time. Reading was my only outlet. Books could take me away from everything. I mostly read fantasy novels, although I couldn't let my dad see them. He thought they were unhealthy."

Sylvie laughed. "I read them late at night, in my room…" She thought about her mom's treatments. "When Mom's pills worked, life seemed almost normal. When she didn't take her medication…" She broke off.

Clearing her throat, she said, "Then, in junior year, your novel, *The Queens*, was assigned in our English class."

Her heart lifted at Alice's smile and she relaxed. "Your writing, like my mom's pills, brought order out of disorder, cleared my mind, gave me focus." She rooted around in her bag and pulled out a ragged hardcover edition of *The Queens*. Pushing it into Alice's hands, she said, "I know this might be inappropriate," her voice was pleading, "but could you sign it? Please."

"Always one of my favorites," Alice said, looking pleased. Alice took the book and the pen Sylvie had clutched in her hand, and scrawled a few words and her signature, gravely handing both back to Sylvie, who could hardly stay in her seat, her excitement fizzing.

"Oh, thank you," she gushed. "This means so much to me. Wow." She swallowed and took a sip of water. Then she continued, "I'd never read anything like it. I was blown away. We studied it for a month and I probably read it six times. Then I started reading about the Tudors and the Stuarts. History came alive. I haunted the library, looking for illustrated books on England, Scotland, and France. I studied old maps, and read biographies." The words were spilling out of Sylvie's mouth. "After we finished studying the book, I hunted down every book of yours that I could find. I read everything and, as time went by, I continued reading anything you published."

"That's very nice to hear, but…"

"I know," Sylvie said. "No real story there. Your books did more than encourage me to read." She took a breath. "They were much more important than that. Every one had a visceral impact. I could feel the gaits of the horses when characters were out for a ride. My heart broke when David Riccio was murdered, and I shook when the casket letters were discovered. Transporting myself to other places, other times made me feel free. I could transcend my confined existence and be another person. Reading your work had an intellectual effect too. Every book, every story, made me want to know more. I researched history, settings, esoteric words. I read about psychology to better understand the personalities of characters. You pushed me in new directions with every novel you wrote. You opened new worlds, gave me new friends, peopled my internal universe.

"When I went to college, I decided to major in history. I was already good at research. Libraries were my refuge, my safe haven." Sylvie grabbed Alice's hand again. "Feeling as if I knew you, I started having conversations with my imagined version of you. Alice, you obviously don't know this but you encouraged me to go to the University of Chicago, apply for an Emile-Boutmy Scholarship to get a Master's Degree in history at Sciences Po in Paris, and gave me the courage to go when I won one."

Sylvie dimly heard grumbling coming from the crowd and Eddie's soothing voice, reassuring the impatient horde. Speaking more quickly, she continued, "While my first love had been Tudor England, your book on arctic exploration refocused my interests. You whispered in my ear that I should apply for the Arctic Circle program, which gave me an opportunity to go to the Arctic with an amazing group of scientists and artists, enabling me to write my first novel, the book I just published, *Cold Death in the North*."

Sylvie said in a confiding whisper, "I'm hoping it will sell well enough that I can give up my day job as a high-school history teacher and write full time.

Now I'm writing my second novel, the first in a series about murders at the court of Francis I." Despite the soft tone, her glee was palpable.

Sylvie tried to discern Alice's reaction, her stomach starting to ache as she wondered what Alice, who looked very tired, thought of her non-story. The ensuing silence disheartened her. "I'm so sorry for taking up your time," she finally squeaked. "Just another gushing effusion. Not really a story. Totally wasting your time. I'll go now."

Alice smiled and reached out a restraining hand. "You remind me of another young writer," she said gently. "I'd love a signed copy of your book."

—— DEBORAH KAHN ————————————————

...is a retired academic who lives in Chicago with her two cats. She writes romantic suspense and is working on her first novel, which she hopes to publish in 2020.

The Yearbook

by Susan Winstead

Saving the high school yearbook was just the start.

19

Sandy grasped Alice's hand. "I discovered my instinct to be a writer quite accidently during my senior year of high school because of the cowardly act of another student, and a creep, and criminal teacher."

"This sounds like a story about survival," Alice said.

"Yes, on many levels," Sandy said.

ε ε ε

During the 1970s, a peculiar incident happened at my high school in Freeport, Illinois. It was a *Friday Night Lights* kind of place—football season was the highlight of the year. If you weren't doing something related to football you could feel really left out. So, I played an instrument in the marching band, and, during other times of the year, I participated in plays, choir, and speech tournaments—the stuff that didn't get much notice because it wasn't sports.

My senior year, I had a hole in my schedule and the guidance counselor recommended taking a journalism class. So I took a class that produced the yearbook. There were a handful of seniors in the class—all girls. Now you would think there had to be more boys interested in journalism, but that was the first of several oddities about the yearbook I was about to discover.

Strangely enough, the other seniors on the yearbook staff belonged to a clique perceived as neither welcoming nor respectful to students who weren't a part of their inner circle. They'd never attend the plays and musicals people like me were in. It was beneath them. They wouldn't be caught dead joining a church youth group, especially one we attended. They simply wouldn't associate with anyone outside of their clique—a clique that had existed since grade school.

A shadow hung over the journalism department as my senior year started. The previous year, the yearbook didn't come out on time. Finally, well into the summer, it arrived. The town's newspaper and radio stations announced the yearbook was ready for students to pick up, but everyone was really disappointed it hadn't been ready at the end of the school year. Blame had been put on the yearbook editor. So, a decision had been made to have co-editors, Ann and Marie, both seniors, to share the responsibility the next school year. But, early in the school year, one of them, Ann, did not pull her weight even though she remained in the class, coddled and excused by Mr. Press, the laziest journalism teacher this side of the Mason-Dixon line.

Marie became quickly overwhelmed by the daunting requirements of creating a yearbook. "You can't just sit there and not do anything, Ann," Marie finally said to her in late October.

"Really? Watch me," Ann said, giving a coquettish smile to Mr. Press, who seemed to enjoy watching the girls fight.

"Mr. Press, we've got to work together or we'll never get the yearbook out, just like last year," Marie said pleadingly.

"I'm sure you'll work something out," Mr. Press said, kicking his feet up onto his desk, waiting to see how Ann would react to Marie's panic.

In December, Marie broke down and begged Ann to help. "I don't want this to be like last year, Ann. Don't you care?"

Ann shrugged her shoulders and went back to her conversation with another student. Meanwhile, Mr. Press leaned against the wall, his arms folded across his chest and a smirk on his face.

Until then, I had stayed on the sidelines, mainly because I was new to the class and the journalism department. But, in the few weeks since the school year had started, I silently assessed lack of leadership as the biggest problem. No one had been given any direction. I'd seen enough.

"Marie, I know Ann's not doing a darned thing and Mr. Press doesn't seem to care. I'd like to help if you'd let me."

I had strong organizational and leadership skills and Marie had technical skills, so we forged a great partnership and the yearbook was soon headed in the right direction. We determined who would spearhead different sections—academics, activities, clubs, sports, class pictures—and what copy and photos needed to be produced. We gave specifics about what to do. The pages of the yearbook began to be created. But, there were big consequences for me personally.

The thing is I didn't anticipate the amount of time the yearbook required outside of the school day. It overtook my involvement in band, chorus, and theater. There wasn't enough time in the day for all the work. We had to meet after school at Marie's house. Sometimes she and I would work so late on a Friday or Saturday night, I would stay overnight. We would fall asleep exhausted and sleep soundly until morning. We'd wake up and do some more work before I went home to shower. Then, I'd go back to her house and we'd work through the day. Her parents were very worried about the stress the yearbook put on her and they appreciated the support I gave. They considered me their child as well.

Though it could have appeared that two students were departing from their social groups to work together for a higher cause—the yearbook—it wasn't perceived as noble at the time. My friends didn't understand. One of them confronted me, complaining I'd become so preoccupied I didn't notice her anymore. And, I confused my lines during the senior class play, throwing off everyone else in a scene, upsetting my fellow thespians. The very minute my friend was blasting me, Marie came walking down the hallway with a hard, determined expression on her face, carrying heavy cardboard containers holding the page layouts for the yearbook. She spent every spare minute she could in her other classes and between classes doing something on those layouts. I remember telling my friend I had become so preoccupied because I needed to protect her from him. Him being Mr. Press, the journalism teacher.

Yes, Marie needed protection from the journalism teacher. I lived in a naïve, small-minded community that assumed a teacher looked out for the best interest of students. Looking back, every year that man did something to sabotage the yearbook, but no one caught on to him.

The rest of the school year, he let Ann, the other editor, off the hook, placing no demands on her and often times she didn't even attend class though officially she was still co-editor. Instead of supporting the effort we put in outside of the school day, he ridiculed us for taking equipment to Marie's home to work overnight. Despite his admonishments, we continued to meet at Marie's house and we plugged along, getting the yearbook pages completed. When we delivered the pages to him so he could send them to the publishing company, he didn't. He sat on them for weeks and didn't bother to proofread them for errors.

Marie feared the yearbook would be late and she'd get the same flak as the editor the previous year. The pressure put her on the verge of a breakdown and the principal and assistant principal didn't pick up on the teacher's treachery.

Who knows what motivated the yearbook teacher to sabotage the project? Marie thought it was some sort of reverse psychology, but I think it had something to do with us being girls. I don't know how else to explain it. To add insult to injury, I was listed as a special assistant to the editor, understating the responsibility I had taken on. Nothing I did had been valued by adults at the school. In fact, the journalism teacher seemed to have contempt for me. Despite all that, the yearbook came out on time and everyone had it in hand before the end of the school year. So, I guess that was all that mattered or so I thought at the time.

$$\varepsilon \; \varepsilon \; \varepsilon$$

Sandy looked up at Alice and shrugged.

"Your story is both happy and sad, but mostly frustrating," said Alice. "What did you do after you graduated? I'm sure the experience affected the decisions you made in your adult life."

"I wanted to leave that place forever," said Sandy, "but I had to be patient and plan carefully. Though I helped to save Marie's health, if not her life, she helped me too. She noticed that I was a voracious reader and natural writer with good leadership skills. She convinced me to pursue my true talents and I did. I went to a community college and graduated before transferring to a university. When I graduated from there I pursued a career in the military where I not only traveled, but lived in Europe. On rare occasions, I'd go back to where I grew up and people from the infamous clique who never spoke to me in high school would express their gratitude for how I helped Marie. The term 'post-traumatic stress' wasn't in use at the time, but we both could relate."

"So, you got some credit for it after all," Alice said.

Sandy smiled. "The happy ending was a long time in coming, but it came. Marie would speak of our situation over the years and eventually the pattern with the yearbook caused the teacher and his perverse abuse to be scrutinized. He modified his behavior and eventually wasn't there anymore. I didn't do much follow-up. I just wanted to put it behind me. What I do know is our experience became a bit of a folk tale of one person helping another."

—— SUSAN WINSTEAD ——————————

…her work has been published in newspapers, magazines, and anthologies and she has won several writing awards. She is past summer program chair, program chair, and president of OCWW. She currently serves as a board member for Jane's Story Press Foundation. She is a native of Chicago, Illinois and a veteran of the U.S. Army.

The Break-In

by Dorothy de Souza Guedes

Lydia's life changes after a cabin break-in.

20

lice needed a break. She'd heard some interesting stories, but most people wanted to talk about her writing, a subject she was not all that interested in exploring. She caught Eddie's attention and motioned him to her side.

"Eddie, be a dear and help me to the lounge. Would you let these lovely people know I will return in twenty minutes or so?" She whispered into his ear.

One woman stepped out of line as Alice passed by.

"Ms. Bainbridge, I've so looked forward to meeting you in person. But I'm afraid I won't be able to wait for you to return," said the woman breathily, struggling to keep up. Eddie was notorious for taking full advantage of his long stride to whisk his grandmother away.

Alice turned to look at the plain, fiftyish woman who was reaching out, holding a small package in her hand.

"Ms. Bainbridge, I've so wanted to tell you how much one of your books has meant to me that I've written you a letter," the woman said.

Alice politely held out a shaky hand and Eddie slowed. The woman smiled up at him, "Thank you."

Alice accepted the package, then watched as the woman hurried away, soon lost in the throng of conference attendees in the hallway.

Eddie expertly backed her into a corner next to a small table. "I'll be off to find you a hot cup of tea, Alice."

Alice closed her eyes, relaxing. Feeling the weight of the envelope in her lap, she sat up, opened the peach envelope, and pulled out the thick sheaf of paper. The high-quality vanilla stationery was filled from edge to edge with beautiful penmanship. Alice unfolded the pages and began to read.

The Break-In

ૅ ૅ ૅ

Dear Ms. Bainbridge:

I'm not much of a writer, but I want to say thank you for writing, *The Queens*. It has meant a lot to me since I was fourteen. I'm not sure where to begin, so I'll jump right into my story.

My name is Lydia Decker. The summer before my first semester as a high school freshman, two neighbors and I began to break into unoccupied cabins that surrounded the lake just north of our small hometown in northwest Illinois. What started out as a one-time dare had, by fall, turned into a habit. Please don't think we were experienced criminals. We were considered good kids, but there wasn't much to keep us occupied in our small town.

Terry and Jimmy, neighbors and best friends since first grade, were two years older than me. We'd become friends the previous spring. Even though I was younger, they accepted me because I taught them a few impressive Frisbee tricks I'd learned from my dad. We'd play Frisbee for hours in the field across the street from my house—Jimmy's house was next door, and Terry lived around the corner—until it was too dark to see.

That summer, I'd gone with Terry and Jimmy a few times to hang out with other high school kids at the lake, but I felt out of place sitting on the pier drinking Pepsis with the long-legged, sophomore and junior girls, so confident in their skimpy bikinis. I was a bit of a tomboy, more comfortable in jeans and T-shirts. I liked it best on those nights it was just the three of us.

I'd begun to feel a new, wild restlessness, an impulsiveness that I'd never felt before. I had moved to the neighborhood the previous spring when my parents separated; my 4-year-old sister Jilly, my mom, and I lived with her sister, my Aunt Janey. My dad was too busy working in suburban Chicago—and spending time with his new girlfriend—to visit.

Because that fall was rainy and chilly, Jimmy, Terry, and I knew most cabins would be closed for the season. Saturday nights, I'd sneak out after Mom and Aunt Janey went to bed; the boys would be waiting around the corner in Terry's restoration-in-progress 1970 Chevelle, lights off. Jimmy had a talent for convincing his older brothers to buy him beer, so we'd usually have a twelve-pack growing warm in the back seat.

Terry would drive to a seldom-used road that ran behind the campground. We'd climb a fence and cross the field that ran along the back of the cabins, then peek in darkened windows until we found a cabin that looked interesting. Jimmy was a master lock picker, and soon we'd be inside drinking beer and smoking.

After the beer ran out one October night, Terry began to open cupboards. Most of the time, we just drank our beer and left everything but games or cards untouched. That night Terry was hoping to find the teenagers' holy grail: hard liquor. He found a bottle of bourbon—if I'm honest, I had no idea at the time that there was a difference between bourbon and any other kind of booze—and we began to pass the bottle around, playing backgammon by flashlight.

Jimmy was antsy that night. He climbed the ladder to the sleeping loft. After a few minutes, he called down to me.

"Hey, Lydie," he called down to me, "you aren't gonna believe what I found!"

As I began to climb, Terry jumped up. "Hey, what about me?"

Terry was right behind me, prodding me and grabbing my ankles as a joke. I hoisted myself into the loft, then walked a few steps to where Jimmy was standing. Terry was next to me in seconds.

In the semi-darkness of the loft, I saw that Jimmy held something in his hands. When I realized what it was, I stepped back, bumping into Terry.

"A gun?" I asked.

"Not 'a gun,'" he mimicked me, "but a rifle."

"Cool!" Terry said, elbowing me aside.

I caught the movement of a bird or bat through the loft's tiny window. As I turned toward it, I felt something, a sort of whoosh, pass by my cheek. At the same time I heard a boom.

The gun had gone off!

Jimmy screamed, "No!" and dropped the gun and the flashlight. He knelt to where Terry had collapsed on the loft floor, almost toppling over the edge. It took a second or two to realize blood was gushing out of a wound in Terry's neck.

I stood, paralyzed with shock until it registered that Jimmy was screaming at me.

"Lydie, Lydie, help me here, Lydie!" Jimmy was crying and screaming, his hands covering the wound, trying to staunch the flow of blood. "Come on, Ter, I'm sorry Ter, hang in there, buddy, hang in there, Ter."

This was in 1979, years before cell phones. None of the cabins had landlines installed. Panicked, I almost fell as I climbed down the ladder. Even though I knew it was unlikely anyone would hear me, I ran outside screaming, "Help, help, help!" I just did not know what else to do.

The rest of that night was a blur. A romantic couple who had snuck out of a nearby church youth group campout heard my screams. The girl ran back to their camp for help, and the boy ran into the cabin. Soon, a church chaperone attempted to stop Terry from bleeding out while another rode his motorcycle to the nearest pay-phone and called the sheriff's office.

Terry was taken by ambulance to the small local hospital. He died within the hour.

That night, sheriff's deputies questioned Jimmy and me separately; they determined the shooting was accidental. The owners of the cabin didn't want to press charges against us for the break-in—much later I learned that they were afraid they'd be sued for leaving a loaded weapon behind—so in a way Jimmy and I got off easy.

But I lost both of them that night. Terry died, and Jimmy and I never spoke again.

Because I couldn't face returning to school, my mom got permission to keep me home for the rest of the semester. I dropped out of my extracurricular activities (theater, choir, class vice president, and volleyball) and refused to speak with friends. All I wanted to do was hide from the world.

And I read. After I read every novel in my aunt's library of paperbacks, I made quick, stealthy trips to the town library during school hours when I'd be least likely to run into anyone. I read anything and everything, hoping for a distraction.

Jenny, the full-time librarian, started to keep tote bags of books she thought I'd enjoy. One day I found a copy of your book, *The Queens*. No book had ever drawn me in as quickly as your story about the Tudors and Stuarts. Your writing was so descriptive, Ms. Bainbridge, it took me to a different world, and I found the escape I'd been searching for since Terry's death. After I told Jenny I enjoyed the book, she began to fill the tote bags with historical fiction. But *The Queens* was my favorite. And it still is.

That December, my parents got back together. My dad told me later that he and my mom were so worried about me that they started talking a lot more and realized how much they missed having the family together. We moved to suburban Chicago—Arlington Heights— and I was enrolled in a small private school.

After Terry died, I found it difficult to maintain friend-ships and spent most of my time alone. My two favorite pastimes were reading and running. For the first time in my life, I became a serious student: *The Queens* had sparked an interest in history and literature and those became my favorite subjects.

There was a shy boy in the class ahead of me who often ran early in the morning when I did. The first few times were a coincidence, but it soon became apparent to me that he was running into me, so to speak, on purpose. Dan was also a serious student and we began to meet in the library to study.

When Dan went to Loyola, I graduated early and fol-lowed him to Chicago. I majored in history for two semesters but never finished my degree. Instead, Dan and I married, and I dropped out to work and support him as he completed his degree. I had our daughter Terri when I was twenty. Becoming a mother brought me out of my shell for the first time since that horrible October night in 1979. Soon, Dan and I were the par-ents of four kids.

Those years were so busy that I hardly had time to myself, so during evening story time, I often read books that I enjoyed to my babies. I read *The Queens* to them so many times that they began to recite passages with me. As they grew older, I let them read aloud the words they knew, then entire passages. My youngest thought the book was written for her because her name was on it: Dan and I had named her Alice, after his grandmother. It was the only time we agreed on a name before the birth of a child.

Only recently did I confess to Dan that I'd wanted to name our daughter Alice because of you.

I wanted to thank you for writing a book that took me out of my sadness as a teen, sparked my interest in history, then became a favorite of my children.

Sincerely,

Lydia Decker

૨ ૨ ૨

Alice dropped the stationery onto her lap and closed her eyes, imagining the pain and loss Lydia Decker had felt.

"Alice? Are you okay?" Alice startled at Eddie's voice. Engrossed in Lydia Decker's story, she had not registered his return.

"Oh, yes, dear. I've just read the most amazing story," she said, looking up at her grandson, her eyes shining. "Isn't it wonderful when someone takes the time to write their story and shares it with others?"

Chuckling, Eddie leaned down and kissed Alice's cheek. "Yes, Alice. Are you ready to return to your fans?"

"Yes, dear Eddie. I feel energized, ready for more," Alice said with a smile that remained until he wheeled her into place at the table. She beamed at the next person in line.

"Thank you for coming today. Do you have a story to tell me?"

DOROTHY DE SOUZA GUEDES

...is a curious and quirky recovering journalist who happily earns her keep as a business content writer. She's proud of her Truffle Bites and not screwing up her adult son (too much). Married to The Nicest Man in the World, Dorothy splits her time between Chicago and Iowa.

The Oklahoman

by Jason Lavicky

William Cordial tries to fit into a new culture.

21

William Cordial spent most of his time in line wondering if he should offer to shake Alice's hand. Didn't women from her generation have to offer their hand first before a man could shake it? Then again, considering she wrote *Revelation, Remorse, and Restitution*, wouldn't it be a bit rude to assume she was still in such an archaic mindset? He didn't want to be rude.

Before William could decide how he would greet her, the line shuffled forward and he found himself looking into the eyes of one of his greatest influences. The shot of admiration was quickly chased by a hint of sadness at just how old she looked. Despite her weak physical appearance, her blue eyes, still alert, showed no sign of dotage. A voice in William's head said, *This is your only chance.*

"Hello, Ms. Bainbridge. My name is William Cordial." He cradled her delicate hand in his, barely noticing how bony her fingers were. "It is such an honor to meet you."

"It's a pleasure to meet you." Her voice, soft and quiet, was almost lost amongst the chattering in the room. William, crouched down in front of her, struggled to isolate her words from the surrounding commotion. He didn't know what to say, or where to start, so he decided to simply cut to the chase.

"Would you sign this for me?" He held up a worn copy of *Revelation, Remorse, and Restitution*. A bit embarrassed by the coffee rings on the cover and the sticky notes peeking out from between pages, William apologized. "My copy's a bit rough around the edges, but, I've gotta say, it's helped me smooth out some rough patches in my life."

Eddie took the book and gently placed it in Alice's lap so she could sign it. "I'd prefer to see it with wear and tear," she said. "That means it's being put to good use."

"Oh, it is. This book has had an enormous influence on me. It even helped me to better appreciate intolerance."

Alice handed the signed book to Eddie, who clapped it closed like a lobster crushing its prey. William jolted upright at the sound. The wide-eyed stares and grumblings from bystanders were palpable, flooding over him, suspending him in place. A beat later Eddie was carrying the book off to the side, luring William away from Alice.

"While I appreciate you reading my book, Mr. Cordial, I'm afraid you completely misinterpreted its message." Her words, though spoken with diplomatic politesse, were punctuated with a thin smile that couldn't hide her annoyance. She turned away as Eddie motioned for the next person in line.

At first bemused, William eventually deduced what was happening and took back his place in line. He drove here all the way from Pittsburgh, and he wasn't about to let the crowd's impatience stop him.

"Sorry. When I say 'appreciate,' I mean that I better understand it. Not that I respect it."

"You should choose your words more carefully, Mr. Cordial."

"Right." William chuckled while adjusting his glasses. "That's why I'll never be a writer." The only thing heavier than Alice's eyelids at this point were the impatient sighs and murmurs behind him.

Get to the point.

I haven't got all day.

He's not even a writer.

"Anyway, I grew up in a small town in Oklahoma. My first summer after graduating college I was offered a job in Pittsburgh. Sure, it wasn't New York or Chicago. This was back in '99, before it was the tech and medical hub it is today. But it was still enough for my parents to think I'd hit the big time. My dad even..."

Before venturing too far off his path and into the thicket of unnecessary details, William noticed Alice's eyelids slowly closing, as if to shield her from any more boredom. He jumped back onto his narrative path, holding up her book. "This book helped me survive Pittsburgh, Ms. Bainbridge!"

Alice's eyes widened and William leaned in closer. "When I moved there, I wasn't ashamed at first to say I had grown up in a small town in Oklahoma. In fact, when I'd go back to my hometown during Christmas, some folks saw me as a big fish in a small pond. I'd finally moved to 'the big city' as my mom would call it."

William paused, and took a breath. He wasn't losing Alice so quickly this time.

"I'm sorry, I'm rambling again. So anyway, there I am in Pittsburgh, and one day they'd invited a speaker to come. He gave a presentation about ways of improving communication within the company. You know, speaking efficiently, effectively, and getting your point across in as few words as possible." William secretly acknowledged the smirk that slithered across Eddie's face. That Eddie could appreciate the irony of the situation actually amused him. The line of people behind William seemed less amused. In his peripheral vision he could see one individual taking a furtive step out of the line to get a better look. Another woman behind him edged her way off to the side of Alice and William, arms akimbo, eyes shooting daggers over her bifocals. A few people, noticeably irascible, began tapping their own books, thinking this would speed up his story.

William continued. "The speaker also addressed facial cues and body language."

Eddie uncrossed his arms and put his hands in his pockets. The impatient spectators suddenly looked away and got back in line behind William.

"He was going on about how fast people from different parts of the country talk. New Yorkers at something like 120 words per minute. Boston at 110 words per minute. Then for no reason, I guess, other than to be funny, he said Oklahomans speak two words per minute. Amused with himself, he laughed, shook his head arrogantly, and followed up with, 'Have any of you ever been there?'

"Everyone in the room turned and looked at me. I heard a few people snicker, but I knew most of them just wanted to see my reaction. It was humiliating. The biggest laugh came from one of the vice presidents.

"The ridicule didn't stop with that incident, though. A few days after that, I had misspoken about something—I can't even remember what it was. And that same vice-president said something along the lines of 'Where are you from again?' So no matter how big I was in that small pond in Oklahoma, I was like toxic algae in the Three Rivers."

Alice and Eddie nodded.

"Needless to say, I didn't get very far up the corporate ladder at that place. And while I remained in Pittsburgh, ashamed to ever say where I was from, I wanted to distance myself from my past. If anyone ever asked, I would just lie and say that I grew up in Chicago."

Alice smiled. William knelt down and moved in closer to her so he could hear her. "Sometimes it takes painful moments like those to help us better understand the world we live in," she said.

"We also have books like yours to help us better understand it and to help us power through those moments with equanimity."

Alice nodded in agreement.

"*Revelation, Remorse, and Restitution* made me realize that I didn't want to spend the rest of my life pretending. I wanted to be proud of who I was and make a difference."

William looked down at the book in his hands and opened it to one of the sticky notes. "You wrote, 'We can't see it, but the future is out there waiting for us, and we shouldn't assume that we can't change what we can't see.'

"That's when I realized that change starts with children. I decided that becoming a teacher would help me shape future generations to be more caring and empathetic. I believe that tolerance is one of the things that will make the future brighter. And while many people today don't see it that way, there's still hope for our children to change that."

William stood up. "There are narrow-minded people even in big cities. That was my revelation. My remorse was trying to forget who I was simply because of that. Now I have kids—a son and a daughter both in elementary school—who have more opportunities than I did at their age. But I also want them to understand that having those opportunities doesn't give them the right to humiliate those who don't have the same opportunities. I'm not ashamed to tell my kids or my students where I'm from. And they don't feel the need to judge me—or anyone—because of that. That's my restitution."

William smiled and closed the book. "So, thank you. While I can't say I really understand why others feel the need to ridicule and humiliate, I can take comfort knowing I, my kids, and my students aren't contributing to it."

Alice nodded gratefully. "People will always make assumptions about others. It's in our nature. But you can rest assured that you've bestowed upon us the chance for a better future. Thank you for your story Mr. Cordial."

William was at a loss for words, so he nodded and shook her hand. Eddie offered his hand and William shook it, too.

"Sorry for rambling," he said to Eddie.

Eddie smiled. "It was worth it."

— JASON LAVICKY ——————————

...is a professional video editor/animator/illustrator by day and a novice writer by night. He only recently started taking writing classes and attending OCWW workshops. Now his days are getting shorter and his nights are getting longer.

The Big Lie

by Patricia Skalka

A childhood lie informs a writer's life.

22

By the time Edna Parsonsky reached the front of the line, Alice was nodding off.

Edna had waited, not always patiently, for her turn to talk to the famous author, and as she approached the diminutive figure, she tapped her gnarled oak cane sharply against the wooden floor. "I waited half an hour for this. You may as well wake up and hear me out," she said.

Alice's eyes popped open. She kept her face neutral and took in the woman who stood before her. Edna was large and unkempt. Her foggy gray hair straggled out from under a burgundy cloche hat. Her breasts sagged beneath a loose caftan kind of dark green dress and her feet splayed outward in a pair of worn Crocs. Alice ran a hand over the lap of her flowered dress and glanced down at her shiny black pumps, which she wore against her doctor's advice. Edna's tone was unfriendly and challenging. But after the obsequiousness of the others, Alice found it refreshing.

"Who are you?" she said.

"Another old lady, like you," Edna said.

Alice smiled. "Are you a writer as well?"

Edna bobbed her head up and down. "Yes, and like you, I got started when I was six. But it's always bothered me, you know."

"No, I don't know. What are you talking about?" Alice said.

"The pretense of it all."

"Pretense?"

Edna cleared her throat. "Yeah, you know, the lies."

"I'm not at all sure I know what you mean," Alice said, her manner crisp.

"The affectation. The untruths that shape our work."

Before Alice could respond, Edna edged closer.

"Do you think I could have a chair?" she said suddenly.

Alice gestured for her to sit in the visitor's chair. Edna took a long minute to settle in.

"It all started the day I snuck under the back porch with my father's flashlight. I wasn't supposed to be there. It was a secret place with a dirt floor and cob webs hanging from the ceiling. I wasn't supposed to have the flashlight either. But it was raining out and I was bored. I was tired of playing *Sorry* with my brother. Then his friend Alan showed up and they went into his room to look at comic books. They made me bring them pretzels and Tang and then slammed the door on me. 'That's not fair,' I yelled. But the door stayed shut."

"You were six?"

"Yes. Roger was two years older than me, and Alan, a year older than that. 'Go ahead, stay in your stupid old room,' I said. 'I'm going exploring.'"

"Ohh, exploring, I like that. What happened then?" Alice said.

"The door opened. 'Where are you going?' Alan asked. I lowered my voice so my mother couldn't hear me from the back room where she was running the sewing machine like she always did, but spoke loud enough to catch my brother's attention. 'The tomb,' I said. That's what we called the space under the porch."

"And?"

"My goody two shoes brother reminded me that the tomb was off limits. 'You can't go there.' he warned."

"'Yes, I can,' I said."

"'It's dark,' he retorted."

"'I know that,' I said."

"How did you know it was dark?" Alice asked.

Edna smiled and explained that once when her father had crawled under the porch to cover a hole in the wall, she'd had to stand in the narrow doorway and hold the flashlight over his shoulder (he was kneeling, she explained) in order for him to see what he was doing. "I know what it's supposed to sound like when a piece of wood is pounded into another and this didn't sound right. It sounded hollow and when I asked him why, he said it was because it was a false wall. 'What's behind it?' I asked, and he said, 'Nothing.'

"Nothing? Then why bother patching the hole? I wondered. I was sure my father was hiding treasure behind the boards. I thought maybe we were secretly rich, not poor like it always seemed."

Alice's eyes widened. "Stacks of gold bars," she said.

"Yes," Edna said, her face flushed. "Diamonds, too. And canvas sacks filled with cash."

"Why would your father hide such wealth?"

"So we wouldn't be robbed and killed in our beds at night."

"Of course." Alice said. "What happened next?"

"I led Roger and Alan downstairs and got the flashlight from the basement. Then I pushed open the door to the tomb and slipped inside. They followed me in. It was dark and spooky and more cramped than I realized it would be with all three of us in there. The wall was higher than I remembered, and I had to hold the flashlight over my head and stand on my tip toes to try and see behind it. I was just about at the right angle when my brother sneezed and bumped into Alan and Alan bumped into me and I dropped the flashlight."

Edna paused for dramatic effect.

"Go on. I assume you retrieved the flashlight and tried again, or didn't you?" Alice said.

"I couldn't!" Edna cried out as if she were a little girl again, back in that tight, black hole. "The flashlight fell behind the wall where none of us could reach it. It must have looped around because it landed light side up and there was just this eerie glow beaming up from the abyss, taunting us. I wanted to cry but I wasn't going to let those two boys know how scared I was."

"Scared of what?"

Edna looked at Alice as if she were an idiot. "My father, of course. We really were poor. I wore my brother's hand-me down shirts and socks, and if we had dessert it was either jello or pudding made with powdered milk. I knew my father didn't have the money to buy another flashlight like the one I'd lost."

"Your father had a temper?"

Edna nodded. "That night when we sat down at the kitchen table for supper, he asked if one of us had taken his flashlight. There was this terrible silence. Then my brother spoke up and said that he hadn't, which technically was true. I knew Roger was waiting for me to admit what I'd done but I just leaned over my mashed potatoes and shrugged."

Edna's voice grew quiet. "That evening, my father looked everywhere for the flashlight and when he couldn't find it, he decided that Alan had stolen it.

"My father never liked Alan. He called him a thief and forbade my brother to have anything to do with him."

"Why didn't your brother say anything?"

"He couldn't. He was never able to stand up to my father."

"So, you cost your brother his friend?"

"Yes, I did."

Alice glanced at the line of people still waiting to talk to her.

"I'm sorry to hear about your unfortunate childhood…. Edna, is it? But why are you telling me all this? What does this have to do with writing?" Alice said.

"Surely you can see where this is going."

"Apparently not."

"Then you're not as sharp as I thought."

"I beg your pardon." Alice's tone was harsh but she waved off Eddie, who'd started to advance toward the visitor. "Explain yourself, please."

Edna settled further into the chair. "That fall at school we had to write the usual what-I-did-during-summer-vacation story and I wrote about the flashlight and the dark hole under the porch. Only I made my brother the villain, the one who'd taken the flashlight, and portrayed myself as the hero, the one who took the blame and saved him from our father's wrath."

Furrowing her brow, Edna leaned closer. "I lied."

"You were a child trying to make up a story."

"Hah" Edna sat back, triumph scrawled across her broad face. "That's exactly correct. I learned to lie so I could write, and I've been lying since. Reshaping reality. Playing with the facts. Revising memories to fit my storyline. Revamping the histories of real people just as I rewrote the history of what happened that summer."

"Nonsense, you created fiction, a story with a basis in reality. That's what novelists do."

"Precisely, and we're all nothing but a pack of liars."

"Don't hoist me on your petard," Alice said, nearly barking. "You told your nasty little lie at the kitchen table, that's where you went astray. That's the lie that counts."

Edna shook her head. "You don't get it, do you? That was the lie I could have taken back if I wanted to. One word to my Dad and everything would have been set straight. But once I committed the lie to paper, I could do nothing to erase it. There it remains for all time, etched in ink for anyone to read. Oh, don't look at me that way. I'm obsessing about something that happened decades ago and my pathetic little saga is long for the trash, you say. Except that it's not. It was chosen as one of the summer's best and included in a bound copy that still sits on a shelf in the school library!"

With alarming agility, Edna pushed up from the chair and whipped out a piece of paper from a hidden pocket. "And now I get an announcement that everything in the library is being digitized. My story will live forever," she said, waving the sheet at Alice.

"Don't you understand?" Edna looked down from her imposing height. "The lies we write live! For all your wisdom, all the books you've published, hasn't that ever occurred to you?"

Alice said nothing.

"No, I guess it hasn't. Well, let me just say this. Think about the stories you've written, the life stories you've twisted into your best-selling novels, the liberties you've taken with secrets that were shared with you in confidence, the friend's dirty laundry you've hung from a fictional character's clothes line. Aren't you even the least little bit ashamed of yourself?"

Alice pulled her shoulders back and leveled her eyes at the woman's bountiful chest. Then she raised her gaze to the panting face that glared down at her. "No, I am not. I am an artist," she said, pronouncing the word *artiste*.

Edna laughed. "You're a bullshit artist, just like the rest of us. And don't you ever forget it." She leaned closer, sprinkling Alice with moist bits of her halitosis-tinted breath as she went on. "Think of the story you most regret writing, the character, you most regret creating. The one where you crossed the line and wished you could take it all back. The one that defamed someone you loved. You know what I mean. You know you've written it. Think of the biggest lie you ever put into words and tell me you're not just a little ashamed."

With that, Edna slammed her cane against the floor, spun on her heel, and stalked off.

"How dare you!" Alice cried out. She raised her voice over the accusatory tap, tap of the cane, but her inquisitor marched on.

As the woman in green pushed through the line, a triumphant smile tugged at the corners of Alice's lightly pinked mouth.

Then Edna disappeared and the smile faded, and Alice began to cry.

—— PATRICIA SKALKA ———————————

...is the award-winning author of the Dave Cubiak Door County mysteries, including the latest *Death by the Bay.* Previously she wrote for Reader's Digest and other national magazines. Skalka joined OCWW in 2009. She belongs to The Authors Guild and Society of Midland Authors and is president of Sisters in Crime Chicagoland.

Dr. Edgar Hochstein

by Emmet Hirsch

The brilliant and arrogant Hochstein isn't all
he appears to be.

23

More than an hour had passed since the award ceremony ended, and still the old woman found the energy to engage each needy soul clamoring for her attention. *Should I just let her be?* Jennifer Mason mused. *No way.* Not after driving all the way from Iowa City, not after staying in a hotel that was too expensive by half because it was around the corner from the conference center, and not now that her turn had finally arrived.

Half a dozen people crowded Alice Bainbridge's table. Jennifer was certain it was as clear to all of them as it was to her, that after an hour creeping forward half a step at a time she had earned her place as next in line. She stepped forward and opened her mouth to issue the salutation she had been rehearsing since the eastbound entrance ramp on I-80.

But what was this? The man standing to her immediate left moved forward at the very same moment!

What an ass! She jostled him to regain her position, but he had already commanded Alice Bainbridge's attention, a charlatan in a two-hundred dollar tie and two-thousand dollar suit. A Rolex rattled conspicuously on his left wrist as he reached over the table to seize Alice's right hand in both of his. Jennifer glared at him. His brows were raised as though in perpetual surprise, an unmistakable sign of a lift. Perfectly aligned veneers, so radiant they might have ruptured the old woman's cataracts, were perched in a too-wide grin. And before Jennifer could open her mouth in protest, he opened his.

"Hello, Ms. Bainbridge, my name is Dr. Edgar Hochstein."

What kind of a person introduces himself to a stranger as "Doctor so-and-so?"

151

Alice squinted at the doctor through her thick lenses, no doubt bewildered by the sudden materialization of this mannequin out of thin air.

Jennifer fumed. *What an outrage!* Alice Bainbridge should not be forced into prolonged exposure to this Dr. Homberg or Huckleberry or whatever-his-name-was. He hadn't come to share anything meaningful. He was seeking to supplement an overabundance of self-importance with a little more validation from the great novelist.

Alice spoke softly. "Thank you for coming to see me…" she began.

The doctor interjected, "I am a full professor at Northwestern University Medical School and have been listed fifteen consecutive years in *Chicago's Top Doctors*. I hold three U.S. patents and have over one hundred fifty scientific publications in leading plastic surgery journals."

What breathtaking arrogance this Doctor Hoggleton possesses!

"How nice for you, Doctor Hinklestein."

Hah! Vindication! The legendary author was obviously irritated. Not only that, but Alice Bainbridge and Jennifer Mason were revealed to be sisters in derision. They had chosen the same subtle and ironic literary device, the mangling of the interloper's name, to express their disdain!

Alice ran her hand over her forehead and closed her eyes, an unmistakable demonstration of her fatigue. When she opened them the man was still there.

Why am I not surprised that he can't take the hint that it's time to leave her alone? Evidently, the good Doctor Humperdinck had an abundance of patience to call upon in the service of his vanity. Jennifer doubted he waited for much else.

"Is there something you would like to tell me?" Alice asked.

He swallowed hard but didn't respond.

"Doctor?"

Still hopeful, the poor darling!

After another pause he spoke: "I thought you might be interested in hearing how all that success is insufficient compensation for my failure of thirty-five years ago."

Alice was quiet.

Jennifer held her breath.

"I graduated high school as valedictorian and was captain of the math team. I was popular and even, believe it or not, had a pretty girlfriend."

Oh, we believe it!

"Everything I set out to do came easily to me. And everyone told me, wherever I went and whatever I did, that I was a leader. So I volunteered for the Marines. I knew serving in the military would be challenging, but I was woefully unprepared for what happened. Everything I tried fell apart for me. I couldn't march in time…couldn't even swing my arms in rhythm with my own feet. In training I couldn't disassemble and assemble my weapon like the other soldiers. I got disoriented on field exercises and found myself facing in the wrong direction. I had an accidental rifle discharge that killed a goose in flight. Soon I was the laughingstock of the company."

He grimaced and his eyes welled up.

"The other soldiers tormented me. They called me a…a…fag, and accosted me in the shower with words and acts that I couldn't bring myself to say out loud even if you asked me to. My intelligence, my verbal skills, all the things I had previously relied upon, were of absolutely no use to me. Had I been a street-fighter I might have made it, but I wasn't, and it didn't take long for hurtful words to be augmented with fists and kicks. The bullies who were atop the social hierarchy in that setting, like alpha wolves, could smell weakness. The other soldiers feared them, and no one came to my defense. Not a single one.

"Anyway, on April 18, 1983, I was stationed at the U.S. embassy in Beirut, one week before I was to return Stateside for discharge, the most miserable period of my life finally approaching its end. I was standing guard outside the front entrance when a suicide bomber detonated a van packed with TNT and ball bearings. It was as if the whole world had suddenly turned to dust. I was struck blind and deaf for I don't know how long, probably half a minute, but it seemed like hours. When my sight came back to me, the first thing I saw was the body of the soldier who had been standing two feet away from me outside the embassy door. His head had been blown fifty meters away and wasn't recovered until the following day. He was one of sixty-three people killed. I had been shielded by a building column. It was a miracle I was spared."

Alice continued to gaze at him in silence. When he hesitated, both Alice and Jennifer nodded.

"I came to my senses pretty quick and understood what had happened. Some of the wounded were screaming and others silently dying all around me. I had been taught a bit of first aid, and I knew that I could start to help save some of them. Instead, I ran." He gulped. "I was afraid the building would collapse onto us, so I headed out into the city. People were streaming toward me—firemen, American and Lebanese and UN soldiers, regular citizens, all coming to help, and I was hobbling as fast as I could in the opposite direction. I didn't realize until later that a piece of shrapnel had shredded my right quadriceps, but I didn't feel the pain and the bleeding wasn't too bad.

"At one point an officer—I think he was a lieutenant colonel—yelled at me as he ran toward the destruction: 'Where are you going, soldier? About face, and do your duty!'

"I ignored him and staggered away, crouching behind some cars that had been upended like matchboxes by the blast. Finally, I stopped shaking enough to stand, and I returned to the embassy. In the confusion no one saw me crawl to the spot in the rubble where I had been positioned, and there I waited to be rescued and treated for my injury.

"After rehab I was honorably discharged and awarded a Purple Heart, an award I can't even bear to look at. I decided to become a doctor, but the truth is, it wasn't to make amends for what I had done—it was to prove to myself that I was more than a coward and a failure. Once I was back in school, the old confidence and success slowly returned. I graduated at the top of my class and had my choice of the best residencies. And I have already shared with you a short version of my résumé since then.

"But it's done no good. It's all a sham. I am, in fact, a coward and a failure, a divorced plastic surgeon whose kids won't talk to him, a man with no friends, lots of material things and not a single possession worth having."

Jennifer felt like she hadn't breathed in minutes. Alice stared at the man and then heaved a deep sigh. Finally, she said, her ancient voice quavering: "What did you say your name was?"

EMMET HIRSCH

...is an obstetrician-gynecologist and research scientist in Evanston, Illinois, and a Clinical Professor of Obstetrics and Gynecology at the University of Chicago. He is author of the novel *The Education of Doctor Montefiore.*

Persistence of Memory
by Joan Naper

Kathy's childhood friendships come alive
in her stories.

24

A tanned, athletic woman who was no longer young approached, holding out her hand to shake Alice's. Alice ignored it.

"Hello, Alice. I'm Kathy Connor. You said that listening to good stories is part of what keeps you alive. I'm hoping that the story I have to tell will take you even further."

Alice gave the woman a tired nod to go ahead.

Kathy gazed off into the distance and began:

ε ε ε

When I was eight years old, I used to sit on top of our garage and watch my big brother Johnny and his friends play basketball in the alley. A little tree—more like an overgrown weed—grew next to the garage. I'd climb up on the fence, climb the tree, and then grab the shingles to pull myself onto the pitched garage roof. My mother hated this. She thought I would fall off and break my leg or worse. If she saw me from the kitchen window, she'd pound on it and yell at me to get down.

I knew Johnny wouldn't tell on me—he thought I was feisty for a girl, and I could tell he was proud of me. But she told him that he had to cut down the tree so I wouldn't climb up there anymore. We both ignored her as usual.

That Saturday morning I remember noticing as I put on my red gym shoes, the rubber soles were nearly smooth—it was time to ask my mother

157

to buy me some new ones. I hated going with her to buy shoes and clothes. She took me to city stores that smelled like old men, and she always bought the cheapest ones. "There are seven of you to buy for," she'd say. "And you all need new shoes every year. Do the math."

I didn't do math—I was in the third grade. I did arithmetic. And I hadn't mastered the times tables yet. But I knew what she meant.

On the garage roof I sometimes sat behind the backboard where my brother and his friends couldn't see me. But I'd usually sit on the sloping side next to it so I could watch them. Of course, they could see me then. Mostly they didn't pay attention to me. But that morning, Johnny saw me and said, "Get down. You're going to break your neck."

"I haven't yet."

"You only have to fall once and you're dead."

"Then I wouldn't care, would I?"

He couldn't argue with that so he went back to playing ball. Just after he made a basket and earned the final E in HORSE—there weren't enough of them to play a full game—he started to dribble the ball slowly. I thought he was getting ready to pass the ball to Tommy, but he feinted and jumped and threw the ball up high onto the roof.

The ball bounced off the roof and back down to the alley. I yelled down, "Can't hit me!"

He kept throwing it and so did his friends when they got the ball. I was really hurt that Tommy was one of those aiming at me. Even though he, like Johnny, was five years older than me, I'd had a crush on him since I was six. Tommy had big blue eyes, a wide smile, and lots of freckles. He looked like Howdy Doody and I loved him.

I wondered if Tommy would ever like me, maybe some day when I was in high school. He'd be an older man then, maybe even in college. But he'd probably wait for me until I was old enough to get married. He seemed like that kind of boy.

I was watching Tommy and didn't notice that Johnny had disappeared. I must have heard the garage door open because I looked over my shoulder instead of where I was gripping the brace of the backboard. My smooth gym shoes started to slide down the gritty shingles of the roof, but I held on tight.

Then Johnny came out of the garage with the little axe in his hand. "I'm going to cut down that tree and you'll be stuck up there forever!" he said. He ran around the yard holding the axe over his head and yelling "Woo, woo," like an Indian on the warpath.

I needed to get to the tree before Johnny could cut it down. I couldn't move very fast because I kept slipping and sliding. It was hard to keep my balance as I tried to climb up to the top and slide down the other side. Johnny taunted me, patting his mouth and shouting his pathetic Indian war cry as he danced around the back yard.

All of a sudden I felt the basketball smack me in the middle of my back. And I slid and fell all at the same time. Was it Tommy who threw it? My hero? After that awful moment of feeling out of control, I thought I could hook my leg around one of the backboard supports but I couldn't get down that low without falling. I was still closer to the alley side of the roof than the yard side. I knew I would hurt myself more if I fell into the alley than if I fell into the yard, but I couldn't move. Johnny might be right, I could break my neck. I think I would care about that, maybe just before I died. It would probably hurt a lot.

I pulled myself up the garage roof by gripping onto the sides of the tar-paper shingles as I climbed. Once I reached the top, I turned my body around and slid on my stomach, feet first, down the yard side of the roof. Before I fell into the yard I grabbed the gutter around the edge. It held me. Beneath me, in the yard, Johnny was yelling, "I'll catch you, I'll catch you." He dropped the axe and ran around with his hands up in the air as if he was going to grab me as I fell. But I hung there, gripping the gutter, for a minute. I looked over my shoulder. It wasn't that far to the ground. I let go and dropped. The impact hurt, I felt like my legs were driven up through my body. But I was all right. I didn't cry.

Johnny's friends ran into the yard, yelling. Tommy even hugged me. For a second. I forgave him. Almost. But I just stood up straight and looked

Johnny in the eye. "I'll chop down that tree," I said. Before he could get it, I grabbed the axe from the ground and marched over to that little tree that was more like a weed. I gave a few whacks and it broke in two. I grabbed the upper half and pulled it. With a crack, it was just a stump.

ε ε ε

"They're all gone now," Kathy told Alice. "Tommy in Viet Nam. My mother before the turn of this century—lung cancer. And Johnny—just five years ago. A brain tumor."

Alice said, "Sorry for your loss. It's good to know your friends live on in your memory."

Kathy wiped her eyes. "Not only that, as long as people remember the stories we tell and the books we write, we aren't gone. Our writing gives us a way to defy death."

Alice looked to one side of Kathy, the sides of her mouth barely lifting up. Kathy stood there, unsure of what to do. Alice then beckoned her to come closer. "Thank you," she said and reached out to shake her hand.

—— JOAN NAPER

...has had a long writing career, working as a writer and editor in educational publishing companies, marketing companies, and in corporate communications. She was a speechwriter for the American Medical Association and director of research communications at Northwestern University. But fiction is her first love.

Beyond Death

by Susan Van Dusen

A woman in black tells Alice a story.

25

Next in line was an older woman fashionably dressed in a flowing black caftan and a long boa of sleek black feathers. In her left hand she carried, rather than leaned upon, a polished wooden cane with what appeared to be the head of a raven. Her bright ebony eyes were set in an ageless, lined face; she could have been eighty, or a hundred, if a day, but with panache. She extended her arm briskly, yet with care, as she shook hands with Alice and sat at her table.

"Hello, I'm Minerva Stone, an aficionado of your writing," she said, in a companionable voice, as though sitting next to a new acquaintance in a train car.

Alice took it all in with a sigh. More plaudits I don't need, she thought.

"But I have something I want to talk to you about. Something missing from your writings, inspirational as they are."

"Oh? I've overlooked an important element of life?" Alice asked, surprised at being criticized, ever so politely, at a first meeting with this woman in black.

"Yes," Minerva responded with great determination. "Your stories are about overcoming obstacles toward living a good life."

"I always thought that was a worthy effort," Alice sniffed and looked inquiringly at her.

"But you have never tackled a good death, the prospect that death may be positive, or what might be beyond that split second between breathing and then not. It's also something," Minerva leaned over and whispered in Alice's ear, "that you and I are both facing any moment."

"I do not fear death," Alice said slowly, reviewing in her head all that she had written before. Minerva was correct. Alice had never written about a "good death or what might lie beyond." She was intrigued. "Tell me your story." She winced, moving forward in her chair so as to hear everything Minerva had to say.

"It started when I was seventeen and dying," Minerva said. "No one knew what was causing the poison in my system. They removed my appendix. They performed exploratory surgeries. One doctor came in, saw an infection in the scar, and immediately cut it away with his scalpel. The pain was hideous. I prayed for release, of course, meaning death, but it was not a positive act, wouldn't you agree?" Minerva asked.

Alice nodded.

"Several infectious disease experts came to see the girl who would not heal. One by one they stuck their fingers up my virginal path," Minerva shuddered, "but could find no answers except for destroying a young girl's innocence.

"High fevers prompted the doctors to strip me and tie me between two plastic ice water rafts, like the ones children play on in pools. The fevers did not abate."

"This sounds very much like overcoming an obstacle story," Alice murmured. She looked beyond Minerva and saw several others waiting behind her.

Minerva continued, "One day at the hospital, my mother, father and rabbi were standing beside my bed looking at me. Suddenly I was not the jaundiced creature lying between the ice rafts. I was looking down at them."

"Looking down, you say?" Alice's sharp eyes pierced Minerva's face.

"Yes. Then I looked around me. I was lying in a meadow filled with the fragrance of fresh green grass, soft yellow and white flowers. Bees buzzed around gathering nectar, but they didn't bother me. A speckled baby fawn and a tiny brown rabbit slept by the side of a stream that burbled by me. Its water was cool, not the harsh coldness of the ice rafts. The sky was full of clouds that took the shape of common, everyday things. It was all so beautiful. All so perfect. I was at peace."

"Then what?" Alice asked. "Did you die? Did they resuscitate you? Is that it?"

"No," Minerva said. "I watched them crying over me, saying prayers, begging God to make me well. My heart ached for their grief. I looked at my meadow and the brook and the animals, and grudgingly decided to return to the body of that sick child. I chose a life of suffering rather than the Eden I had found."

"So you're here. How does that prepare you for a good death?" Alice queried.

"I learned that death is a wonderful place, not a black abyss to avoid," Minerva's black eyes glowed. "I look forward to the peace of that magical scene again. Yet, in your copious writings you have never even contemplated what wonders exist beyond the kiss of death."

"Well," Alice bristled, "if you believe all that, why are you still here?" She did not remove her rheumy eyes from Minerva's face.

"I was not ready for a good death then." Minerva sighed. "But, it seems, someone else was. While I was ill, my grandmother, the most beloved person in my life, fell and broke her hip. She was in another hospital. As I got better, she got worse. I became cranky because my mother was spending less time with me. She hadn't told me about my grandmother. She was afraid it would set back my recovery.

"On the day I was released from the hospital, Grandmother died." Minerva's eyes turned to granite, taking Alice aback. "I knew then that a deal had been struck between my grandmother and God. I could picture her sitting in her rocking chair with her tightly curled grey hair and red cheeks, wearing her faded yellow apron, talking to Him. 'Let her live,' she was saying with a smile. 'She's young, smart. She'll make something of herself. I've had my time.'"

Minerva closed her eyes and spoke in a monotone. "My grandmother gladly chose death for my sake. She went willingly, so I could remain on earth." Minerva opened her eyes and gently took Alice's hand again. "That," she announced, "was most definitely a positive death."

"Of course," Minerva added, "I told my mother what had happened. Of course, she thought I was crazy. Of course, I was quickly sent off to the psychiatrist. And, of course, I quickly learned to keep my grandmother's deal with God a secret in my heart where it still remains."

"And?" Alice asked.

"And, I have lived my life keeping my grandmother in mind always. She was a kind, giving person, so that is what I have tried to be, though sometimes it goes against my nature. I have travelled to unbelievable places, written books, and now am here with you. But I sense from your most recent work that perhaps you are becoming somewhat bored with life. I want to tell you that what comes after is soft and gentle, something to look toward. And, while you're still here, maybe I can regale you with some more exciting adventures of what is to come."

Minerva's hand reached into a tiny black designer bag by her side. Alice swore she heard the crackling sound made by piles of fallen leaves as children and adults joyously rolled over them. The image vanished when Minerva placed a business card into Alice's hand. "I'd love to visit you soon," she said, standing up, then stooping down to kiss Alice's forehead. "I can bring tea and cakes and tales for you," she whispered, "and anything else you would desire, too."

Alice watched Minerva walk away, back straight, black caftan gracefully flowing, polished cane swinging jauntily from her hand. This time she knew the raven's eyes were staring at her.

"I wonder what she meant by 'anything else you would desire…'" Alice pondered, with a frisson of excitement she could not explain.

"Eddie," she said, handing the card to her grandson, "keep this. I've a feeling we'll be seeing Minerva again," then Alice turned to the next reader who would wish to bend her ear.

SUSAN VAN DUSEN

...is an award-winning writer of editorials and magazine articles. She has written three history books for children, and *The Synagogue: A Home for the Jewish People*. She is currently working on a series of cozies based on a Torah group, and is a member of OCWW, Chicago Writers Association and Sisters in Crime.

Tango

by Judy Panko Reis

An unreliable friend needs one last favor.

26

Alice sighed. The line, at last, was gone. Her day was almost complete.

Then, in large, red glasses, Jill Nagel appeared. With an internal growl, Alice took her former protégée's hand. The memory of Jill's betrayal fifty years ago scorched her brain. *The nerve! Wasn't hustling me out of the book deal enough? And never an apology.*

Alice's startled eyes met Jill's smile.

Doused in Chanel, Jill wore a neon paisley blouse reminiscent of psychedelic wallpaper. Crowning Jill's blondish gray hair was a towering red feathered hat. Poised in front of a parade of Alice's admirers, the seventy-five year old Jill resembled an aged drum majorette.

Jill could kick start the dullest of parties by starting a conga line. Her passions blazed contagious and were a driver of her success as an author. It was said that, as a writer, Jill could hook a white shark with the turn of a phrase.

During Jill's graduate days, a collegiality emerged between Jill and her instructor. Under Alice's tutelage, Jill published her first fiction piece, "Snakes in the Grass." The achievement prompted Alice to network Jill to agents and publishers who deemed her a writer most likely to surpass her mentor's notoriety. The creative sympatico that colored their efforts for years fueled mutual success. Until Jill goaded Alice into a book collaboration on which Jill reneged, leaving their friendship estranged.

For all the tensions between them, there was a loveable side to Jill, too. She could be big-hearted and she was a brilliant novelist. But Jill's dark side included a selfishness that had inflicted humiliation on Alice.

Alice wasn't alone in becoming collateral damage to Jill's constant pursuit of the next shiny object. Her three ex-husbands and opioid-addicted daughter were evidence of that. Like Alice, they had all been seduced by Jill's magic. *Come here, come here. I need you, I want you, and I love you.* And then, *Get away,* as she shoved people out of her life. This was the tug and shove tango with which Jill ensnared anyone who was drawn into her aura.

Relief came with a gaggle of undergrads armed with paper thin tablets and gargantuan backpacks. They clustered around Alice, pushing Jill aside.

Alice was a mark for budding writers, eager to grant their requests for autographs, and for a privileged few, gems of writing wisdom. Mentoring students was a perk of her writing career. There was nothing that she craved more or found more gratifying. *With the exception of mentoring Jill Nagel.*

When the last selfie was shot and autograph signed, Alice scanned the room, calculating her next move. *I'm here for today's students, not traitors of yesterday.* Alice imagined Jill evaporating in a poof.

No such luck. While student volunteers retrieved loose programs, Alice spied a crowd of faculty and literati squealing in delight as they huddled around the crimson feathered, Jill, who was in her element holding court.

Alice grimaced. Jill pranced toward her then tripped and stutter stepped to regain her balance.

"So where were we, Alice, You look terrific!"

"It's been, what, fifty years?" Alice's eyes widened. "Such a surprise, what brings you to Evanston?"

"I moved into an assisted living place on Ridge and saw the posters about your award in the lobby. I am thrilled to reconnect with you after all these years." Jill's voice quivered.

Alice wondered if the tremble she detected in Jill's voice was a sign of her desire to make amends for her betrayal.

"Yes, after all these years…" Alice averted her eyes from Jill to summon Eddie. It was time to go.

But Eddie was oblivious, engulfed in a deep discussion with a tall, long-haired co-ed.

Seizing the moment, Jill inched closer to Alice. Alice was overcome by the scent of the Chanel and caught off guard when Jill planted a tissue-wrapped bundle in her lap. With a hoarse whisper Jill leaned into her right ear.

"Alice, I desperately need to talk with you before you leave. It's urgent."

The request puzzled Alice. Why here and now? Was Alice finally about to get the apology Jill owed her? Or was it something else?

Why should I give her an ear? She'd never do the same for me. Denying Jill would be an act of self-preservation, not revenge. *But I'm Not Jill.* Alice's face relaxed when she permitted herself to indulge her default for civility.

"I can give you three minutes, no more." Alice recruited a student in a Northwestern sweatshirt to wheel her to the enclave near the fire exit.

Jill sat herself opposite Alice.

"It's so kind of you to see me." Jill removed her glasses and gnawed on the tip of the red plastic arm.

Alice opened herself up to hear the apology she felt was coming. Jill's eyes narrowed and her voice softened.

"Listen Alice, I know I've made mistakes that disappointed so many of my friends and colleagues, but life has a way of teaching us the lessons we need to learn. I'm learning mine."

It wasn't an apology. Alice remained rapt to Jill's voice which trembled as it had earlier. Alice noticed Jill's unsteady hands when she unzipped her purse, fumbling to raise a tissue to her nose. So as not to stare, Alice glanced toward a student studying her cell phone.

"I'm sure you're wondering why I'm here. I confess, I'm here for a favor."

Alice suppressed her alarm at the absence of an apology and the audaciousness of Jill coming here with her hand out. *Typical Jill.* Alice's face burned.

"The truth is, Alice, I've been losing function in my limbs for some time. I'm living with the degenerative effects of a neuromuscular disorder which is why I moved into the assisted living apartment. Worse, I'm battling an emotional darkness that is suffocating me."

Alice listened to this writer, twenty five years her junior, describe a quality of life far inferior to her own.

"I'm ashamed to admit it, but I'm losing my ability to write. I can't grip a pen. Executing strokes at a keyboard is impossible. It's killing me." Jill suppressed sobs.

"I've tried voice recognition software but that's complicated by my voice tremors. I'm terrified that my thinking and memory are not what they used to be. It's enough to make me want to put an end to it all."

Alice closed her eyes in sympathy but remained mindful of their past. "I'm so sorry to hear of your challenges. How can I help?"

"I'm under contract to finish a book this year. You're the only writer I can trust to help me deliver. The story draws on my admiration for you. It needs some work. I'd make it worth your while."

Alice's body stiffened. *No way!* She marveled at Jill's hubris.

"I know it's a lot to ask, Alice, but with my loss of function and memory, you're my last hope. I know we have some history. Don't feel pressed to give me a decision today. What do you think?"

Caution edged into Alice's response. She was careful not to commit. "Let me give it some thought."

Jill wiped her eyes, hugged Alice, and released a yelp.

"Don't forget my gift for you! It's not much. A token of my appreciation honoring our university days together." Alice reflected on Jill's penchant for bearing trivial gifts in exchange for huge favors from friends.

"Thanks, Jill. Best of luck to you." Jill left.

When Alice unwrapped the gray/purple Northwestern pom-pom hat, it sparked a surge of adrenaline and an uneasy grin. She pulled a mirror from her bag. Momentarily she was transported back to the zeal of her graduate days. "Wow, that's not bad. Go Wildcats!"

Beneath the pom-pom and memories of Jill's *Snakes in the Grass* heyday, simmered a nagging voice: *Fool me once shame on you, fool me twice...*

— JUDY PANKO REIS ————————————

...has published numerous papers and textbook chapters in the area of health care policy for people with disabilities. Her personal essay, *Under the Volcano,* was published in *Shambala Sun* magazine in 2015. A member of OCWW since 1989, she has hosted a critique group for the last six years.

Alice Goes Home

by Jay Rehak

Alice reflects on all she has learned
at the conference.

27

lice waved at Eddie as Jill left the table. The co-ed talking to Eddie gave a look of disappointment, then walked over to apologize to Alice.

"I'm sorry I took so much of his time. It's just that Eddie's so interesting."

Alice looked at Eddie in a grandmotherly way and said, "Yes, my grandson's a real charmer. I'm sorry I have to drag him away from you, but I'm tired and it's time to leave."

Eddie blushed a little, both at the young woman who had no idea or interest in who his grandmother was, and also at Alice. He had been attentive during some of the stories, but listening wasn't Eddie's greatest skill. He much preferred to talk.

"It's nice meeting you, Susan," Eddie said as the twenty-something shook his hand, smiled and walked away.

"You're fifty years old, Eddie," Alice said when the student was outside of earshot.

"She wanted to talk," Eddie offered.

"About what?"

"Something about her parents not respecting her life choices. I don't know. I did most of the talking."

"You know you might just learn something if you listened more. Let's go home."

"Great. I'm starving. Was that Jill Nagel you were talking to at the end?"

"Yes."

"That selfish…"

"Don't say it."

"Did she apologize?"

"No. She wants me to finish a book she wrote. Health issues prevent her from doing it on her own."

"Of course, you turned her down."

"No, I just listened."

"Why?"

"Lifelong habit, I guess. May as well keep an open mind."

Eddie shook his head. "Why?"

"Let's just get out of here."

As Eddie wheeled her out of the Hall, he asked her about the stories she had heard and if she had been moved by any of them.

"Oh, my God, yes," Alice said. "So much pain. Every time I come to these events, I think of the *The Rime of the Ancient Mariner*.

"Remind me."

"Coleridge?"

Again Eddie had a blank look on his face.

"It's an epic poem about a sailor who kills an albatross for no good reason and spends the rest of his life stopping one out of every three people he meets so he can tell them the story and be *temporarily* relieved of the pain of the experience."

Eddie still didn't understand.

Alice continued. "Everyone needs to tell their story. By letting it out, vocalizing it, or writing it down, everyone feels better, for a little while. Then the pain comes back and we have to tell it again."

"I don't need to tell anyone my stories," Eddie said.

"So what were you talking to that young girl about just now?"

"I was telling her about getting thrown out of Rutgers Law School twenty-five years ago."

"Did she ask you about it?"

"Okay, okay, I get it. It just takes me a minute, that's all."

Eddie stopped pushing the wheelchair. He looked around and saw what he was looking for. "I have to go to the bathroom before we get out of here. Let me push you somewhere you won't get bumped and I'll be back in a minute."

"No problem. But I'll probably be asleep when you get back," Alice said, as Eddie wheeled her against the wall, near the entrance to the men's washroom.

As he left her, Alice closed her eyes and thought about all she had heard that day. There was so much to digest. Yes, she was exhausted, but she was also exhilarated. It had been worth the effort to sit and listen, as it always seemed to be. Alice marveled at people's abilities to open up. The women and men who had suffered abuse and had been wounded by relationships. The young woman who had had the affair with the married man, the transgender woman who had learned to "kill" those who had bullied her growing up. The racism the woman from Stanford had endured because she didn't recognize what a phallic symbol was. The woman mistreated by her drug addled, controlling boyfriend. The pacifist who spent years beating herself up for a childhood moment of anger. All of these stories echoed in her mind, and she felt sadder and wiser for hearing them, even as she fell more in love with living than ever.

Still, she was extremely tired. She drifted to sleep and slumped in her chair. Almost immediately, a writer who had been walking by ran over to her, fearing that she might be in distress.

"Excuse me, Ms. Bainbridge, are you all right?" It was Erin Neuman, one of the authors Alice had spoken to less than an hour before.

Oh, yes, dear, I was just dozing," Alice said.

"I thought maybe…"

"You thought I had stopped breathing. I understand. It's why my grandson tries to never leave me alone when we're out in public. As soon as I drift off, someone feels compelled to call 911."

"Well, thankfully, I didn't do that. I was just checking."

"I'm fine, dear. Just tired," Alice said.

"Do you mind if I wait with you until your grandson comes back?"

"Yes, if you'd like and you have the time."

"I do."

"You're the author who recognized the pain in my face when I was thinking about my experience as a six year old, aren't you?"

"Well, I saw the pain in your face, but I didn't know what it was from," Erin said.

"Would you like me to tell you the story?"

"Only if you want me to hear it," Erin said.

"I do. I was six and I'd written my first book," Alice began. "It was handmade out of construction paper and held together by yarn, and, of course, I had no publisher. It was just something that I had started to do when I'd l first learned how to write. I called it *Alice's Silly Book* and I had written short stories, more notes really, about silly things that had happened to my friends and me in our short lives. One day I told my friends about it, and they demanded to see it. Sort of not believing me, and also somewhat concerned, I suppose, that they might be in the book or not in the book, for that matter. When I went home, I quickly added a few notes and returned to my friends, determined to prove to them that I had, indeed, written a book. When they saw what it was written on and how it was bound, they laughed and laughed. Then, they each took turns tearing it up until it was in shreds on the ground. Embarrassed, I laughed with them. They all seemed to think what I had done was foolish, and as I looked at the remnants of the colored paper and yarn scattered on the grass, I was somewhat ashamed of myself and somewhat ashamed of my friends for making me feel ashamed. Of course, it wasn't foolish, it was just something a little girl did to amuse herself. I've relived that story thousands of times in my head, and, to be honest, I've rarely ever mentioned it to anyone. It feels good to tell you now."

Erin rubbed her eyes and looked at the old woman. She bent down and hugged her and whispered, "I wish I could have been there. I wouldn't have laughed. I would have protected you and that book."

"Thank you, dear," Alice said, tears in her own eyes. "I believe you would have. We writers have to stick together."

"Yes," Erin said, just as Eddie was coming out of the bathroom.

Eddie looked at the two tearful women and asked if everything was all right.

"Yes, Eddie," Alice said, "Erin and I were just going over old wounds."

Eddie was about to talk about his own old wounds when his cell phone went off. It was Jamie Ranier.

"Hello?" Eddie said into the phone, pausing. "I understand. I'll be right there." As he put his phone back in his pocket, Eddie explained, "It was Jamie Ranier. She says you accidentally forgot your plaque and I should run back and get it. I wanted to tell her that it was okay with you if…" Eddie looked at Erin and continued, "…if they mailed it to you, but she said it would be better if I could come get it now."

"I can wait with Alice, Eddie," Erin said.

"Great. Thanks, I'll be back in a minute."

Just as Eddie left the two women, Jamie Ranier came walking towards them. She was a considerable distance away, but she was moving as quickly as she could, cradling the precious plaque.

Eddie walked quickly to meet Jamie halfway.

"Thanks," Eddie said, when Jamie handed it to her.

"No problem," Jamie said, "I'm sure Alice wouldn't want to leave without it."

"No, I'm sure she wouldn't want to do that," Eddie said. "Great conference by the way. Alice met a lot of great writers."

"Glad to hear it. We're hoping Alice will come back next year."

Eddie smiled and nodded. "You know she'd love to come back if…" Before he could finish his sentence, Eddie heard a loud scream. He turned and saw a rush of people surrounding Alice's wheelchair. Eddie and Jamie raced to the commotion. When they arrived, a number of people were on their cell phones, each calling 911. In the middle of the conference attendees sat Alice, motionless and apparently not breathing.

"Alice," Eddie pushed his way through the group until he was next to his grandmother. He said, as if part command and part plea, "Stop it, Alice! Come back. Come back."

By the time the paramedics arrived and packed her into the ambulance, it seemed clear that Alice was gone. Tears were running down Eddie's face as he climbed into the ambulance beside his grandmother. "Not yet, Alice, not yet."

He kept talking to her, whispering in her ears, then shouting at her, then sort of speaking to himself.

The EMT personnel kept checking Alice's vital signs and didn't seem to offer much hope.

Eddie looked down at his grandmother one last time and said, "Come on, Alice, not yet, not yet. Please."

A sudden beep of the heart monitor broke the silence.

Alice's eyes flickered and she said, "I feel bad for Kathy."

"What?" Eddie said, wiping the tears from his face, grateful Alice was alive, but wondering what form of delirium she had fallen into.

"She loved Tommy, but he was throwing basketballs at her while she was on the roof. She could have been killed. I mean, 'you only have to fall once and you're dead.'"

"What?

"It's' from a story I heard today. I must have heard twenty-five. I'll tell you all of them when we get home."

And she did.

JAY C. REHAK

...created the storyline for *A Reason to Be Here*. He is the co-author of numerous crowd source novels including: *30 Days to Empathy* the world's first high school class sourced novel. His comedic plays have been produced around the world; his *10 Short Plays You Need to Read Before You Die* is available on Amazon or by visiting www.sidelineinkpublishing.com. Jay is currently writing *Sideline & Company* the third novel in his middle grade *Sideline* series. He invites everyone to visit his website www.laughsaver.com and record a bit of their laughter.

About Jay Rehak

Jay Rehak has been a teacher for thirty-four years. He is the author of the hit middle grade novel series, *Sideline*, the story of a twelve-year-old entrepreneur who secretly builds a fortune while helping her dysfunctional family survive. Jay has written twenty-seven short produced plays, and has authored or co-authored ten novels.

In 2013, Mr. Rehak created and co-authored the award winning *30 Days to Empathy*, the world's first high school class sourced novel. His book *How to Write a Class Sourced Novel* is widely used in high schools throughout the United States, and his TedX Talk on the subject of creating empathy through collaborative writing can be seen at: http://bit.ly/TedXRehak.

Subsequently, he and his students wrote four versions of *Someone Else's Shoes* as well as four versions of *The Absolutely Awesome Adventures of Internet Ed* (available on Amazon.com). Jay is also the producer of WYDUBTV, a weekly news and variety show which can be seen at www.wyoung.org.

He is married to award-winning children's singer, Susan Salidor. He has three children, Hope, Hannah and Ali. Additional biographical information can be found at www.sidelineinkpublishing.com.

Made in the USA
Middletown, DE
02 May 2019